Kissed by Destiny

Sunwalker Saga: Book 8

Shéa MacLeod

Kissed by Destiny
Sunwalker Saga: Book 8
Text copyright © 2016 Shéa MacLeod
All rights reserved.
Printed in the United States of America.

Cover Art by Amanda Kelsey of Razzle Dazzle Designs
Editing by Theo Fenraven
Formatted by PyperPress

Dedication

In memory to friendships lost by the wayside
Whether for good or ill.
There will always be a hole in our hearts.

Prologue

"Something's not right."

"Kabita?" The caller ID on my cellphone had shown a number in the United Kingdom. It had to be her, but the words were garbled, and the line buzzed with static.

"Of course, Morgan," she said with a snap of impatience. Typical Kabita. "Who else would it be?"

Kabita Jones was my best friend and my boss at the private investigation firm in Portland, Oregon where I worked. Our real job was less about stalking straying spouses and more about hunting vampires, demons, and other monsters, but cover stories are important if one doesn't want to freak out the locals.

After the death of her father, Kabita had returned to her hometown of London, England to spend time with family and straighten out the mess Alister Jones had wreaked before his death. At first she'd called or emailed every day, but the longer she was abroad, the less frequent the contact. I'd tried not to worry, with limited success.

"You're breaking up. Can you call me back?"

"No time."

"Where the hell are you? I haven't heard from you in over a week." Actually, I hadn't heard much from her before that. Ever since her father had turned traitor, and she'd gone off to London to clean up his mess, communication had been sorely lacking. Brief emails and texts were about all I could expect, so a phone call out of the blue was a welcome if unexpected treat.

"Not important." Her voice crackled through the line. "I don't know for sure what's going on, but I'm looking into it."

"Um, okay. What can I do?"

"Nothing. Just stand by in case I need you."

"Sure thing, but—"

"Good," she interrupted.

The line went dead. I stared at my phone with exasperation before shoving it back in my pocket. I guess she'd call when she needed me.

Chapter 1

"Kabita is dead."

I sat behind my desk, blinking like a freaking idiot. My mind was completely blank. Nothing there. Zero, zip, nada. Just a faint humming like when the TV goes all black-and-white spots and there's nothing but static.

Yeah, that was it. My brain was static. I couldn't have heard right. It was a mistake. A bad dream.

I focused on the painting hanging next to the door. The splashes of vibrant color were stimulating. That was real. A real, solid thing. This information about Kabita? Not real. Couldn't be.

I laughed, and I heard the slight edge of hysteria. "This is a joke, right?"

Trevor Daly, my brother and handler from the SRA — the Supernatural Regulatory Agency — heaved a sigh and sank back in the faux leather visitor's chair. His skin was gray from exhaustion and grief, and there were dark circles under his eyes. He looked like hell.

"No, Morgan. I'm sorry. I wish it was, but our counterparts in British Intelligence found her body."

MI8. He meant MI8, the agency Kabita had once worked for. The one she'd gone to clean up. They were the British version of the SRA responsible for apprehending criminals of the non-human variety.

"I don't want to hear this." I stood up so fast, my chair toppled over with a clatter against the hardwood floor. I never used my office at the private investigation firm where I worked with Kabita and my boyfriend, Inigo Jones, but Trevor had asked for a meeting that evening and it seemed super official, so the office it was. Now I was wishing it had been a bar. Only I couldn't drink.

Dammit.

Bile worked its way up my throat. Not again. I'd been puking all damn morning.

"Hold that thought," I muttered and dashed out of the room. I could vaguely hear Trevor calling my name, but I ignored it and slammed the bathroom door shut. I didn't bother locking it, just dropped to my knees in front of the Great Porcelain God.

Nobody had told me how much being pregnant sucked donkey balls.

And nobody told me that losing your best friend hurt so bad, it was like your insides were being torn out by a demon's talons.

Once I was done puking, I sagged against the bathroom wall and stared blankly at the gray tile floor. Little black spots danced in front of my eyes. The white noise was back. So many questions, but none of them could surface. It was too much.

Inside me the Darkness rose, unchecked. I didn't bother to stop it. I threw my head back and let it howl until I didn't have an ounce of strength left. Then I lay there on the cold floor, eyes dry, wishing like anything I could cry.

The bathroom door edged open, and Trevor poked his head in, brown eyes filled with concern. "Morgan?"

"Leave me alone."

"I don't think so." He pushed his way inside. "You don't look so good."

"*Pppht.*" I gestured dismissively.

"You don't smell so good."

I glared at him before staggering to my feet, then glanced at the tiny bathroom window high up in the white tiled wall. It was nearly dark. "Don't need to smell good to hunt a vampire."

"You can't hunt in this condition."

I gave him a look that would have quelled a weaker man than him. "Try and stop me."

# # #

The back of my skull throbbed with the strange gripping sensation that told me a vampire was near. I carefully slid my sword from the sheath against my back. And...

Leaned over and puked my guts out.

When I finally stopped heaving, I looked around, confused. I remembered getting in my car, but the rest was a blur. It was dark, but the stylistic streetlamps lining the walking path next to the Willamette River gave me a clue. I was in the middle of Waterfront Park in downtown Portland, and I didn't remember how I'd gotten there. The last thing I remembered was the news...

I shoved the thought out of my mind. I was committed. Kabita would want me to keep fighting. Besides, fighting vamps meant I didn't have to think about her being—

I saw something move from the corner of my eye. A flash of deeper darkness against the night. Sword still gripped tight in one hand, I spun to face the vamp. She was over six feet tall and muscular— practically an Amazon—her hair a wild halo around her face. Her full lips were pulled back, revealing sharp, yellowed fangs. She was an old one, her skin ashen from the centuries. Her age pressed on me, and I heaved again, gagging. Dear gods, what was wrong with me?

She sneered. A sound of derision hissed between her fangs. She strolled toward me, swaying her hips like a runway model. Her eyes were pools of black in the moonlight. "A pregnant hunter. How delicious." The *S* was sibilant. I half expected her tongue to flicker out like a snake's.

How did she know? Scent, maybe. Vampires had a keen sense of smell, like animals scenting prey so they could weed out the weak, the sick, and, apparently, the pregnant. Goody.

I bared my teeth. Not as scary, since I lacked fangs, but it was all I had the energy for.

The vampire let out a grating laugh. "Come, Hunter. Dance with me."

She beckoned me with one long finger. Damn, the woman had big hands. She shook dark hair out of her face and circled me clockwise. I didn't move. I didn't have the energy to waste. I needed to put her down and put her down quick. Maybe this hunt hadn't been such a good idea after all.

The Darkness howled to get out. It was edgier these days. Wilder, lonely perhaps, with the other powers gone. Angry that I refused to use it. I was worried about what it would do to the peanut, although admittedly it had risen unbidden more than once and the peanut seemed fine.

My pain fed the Darkness and the Darkness loved it. It wanted to fight. To feed. I pushed it down. No sense tempting fate.

The vampire danced in too close, and I whipped down my sword with hunter speed, slashing the flesh of her lower arm to the bone. Dark, thick blood oozed from the wound. She screeched in pain and rage, but it didn't stop her. Didn't even slow her down. She rushed forward and hit me like a linebacker.

Air whooshed from my lungs as I flew back, tumbling head over feet across the park lawn. I rolled onto a hard surface and came to a halt a few feet from the Salmon Street Fountain. My cheek was pressed against cold concrete, and little bright spots flashed in my vision. With a groan I hauled myself to my feet. Every joint in my body ached.

I turned in time to see her fly out of the darkness, clawed hands extended. She'd have ripped half my face off if I hadn't ducked out of the way. She flew over my head and splashed into the fountain with an ungodly screech. The Darkness in me laughed. It loved this little game of cat and mouse.

I stalked toward her, blade in hand. She was trying to slosh her way out of the water, but the spray kept hitting her in the face. Every time she'd hiss like a cat.

I took advantage of the situation and rushed in, ignoring the damage to my boots. I swung my blade. She dodged, but I slashed her thigh, flaying it open like I'd fillet a fish. The edges of skin and muscle hung loose, and the bone was white in the lamplight. Ew.

I heaved again, but this time it was dry. I wasn't sure whether to be thankful or not. My diaphragm spasmed. My stomach was so sore, I could barely stand up straight. My moment of distraction cost me.

The vamp raked her nails across my upper arm, drawing blood. The pain was sharp and instant. I snarled, irritated I'd let her land one. Dammit, I needed to pay better attention. Fury welled, and I channeled it into one, solid thrust of blade through the chest wall. The sword cracked through rib and pierced her heart. The vamp's eyes widened a split second before she burst into ash and dust.

I stared at the innocuous little pile lying on the grass of Waterfront Park. It was so innocent. How could something so harmless have once been a bad-ass vampire? I scuffed the toe of my boot across it, scattering it into the ground. Just in case.

And then I leaned over and vomited again.

I sank onto the grass as the white noise returned. Resting my head on my knees and pressing the heels of my hands to my temples, I willed tears to come, but my eyes remained dry. I needed to cry. Why couldn't I cry?

I don't know how long I sat there, but after a while I realized someone was sitting beside me. Someone who smelled of campfires and chocolate. I'd know that scent anywhere.

"Kabita—"

"I heard," Inigo said softly, wrapping an arm around my shoulders. He was oh so warm. He soothed me in a way no one else could.

"I'm sorry," I said, sounding a little strangled. "You must be so upset." He and Kabita had called each other cousins. In actuality, she'd been a much more distant relative, but she'd also been his handler for years. They'd worked together for over a decade. They'd been close.

He was quiet for a moment. "I've lost many people I love over the centuries. Each time it nearly ripped me apart until I couldn't bear it anymore. I had to learn to deal with it. It still hurts, but after four hundred years I manage it differently."

I was surprised he was so calm about it, but it made sense. "Maybe you can teach me."

"Maybe in a hundred years or so," he said wryly.

I had no idea if I'd even live another hundred years. Could be less or a lot more thanks a weird quirk of genetics. I didn't dwell on it much.

"Do you know...?" I swallowed. "Do you know what happened?"

"Only what Trevor knows. They found her in the River Mersey near Liverpool. They have no idea how she died. There was no sign of trauma."

"It wasn't a demon or a vampire or something?" I would have expected her to go out that way. Fighting the bad guys to her last breath.

He shook his head. "Not unless the monsters have found a way of killing that leaves no mark."

Unlikely. Vampires cared for nothing but blood and would rip a victim to shreds to get at it. Even those in more control would leave marks. A demon?

Well, they'd be more likely to turn you into slime. There would definitely be signs.

"What was she doing in Liverpool? I thought she was working with MI8 in London." Undoing the mess that was her father's evil legacy. Alister Jones had been a very bad man.

"That's what we all thought, but Trevor talked to one of her brothers. Turns out she disappeared from London a week ago. They had no idea why or where she'd gone."

A week ago. Right about the time she'd called me. I rubbed my face. There was a lump in my throat the size of an ostrich egg, but the tears still wouldn't come. And I was feeling queasy again.

"I'm going to find out what happened," I said, half expecting him to argue. He didn't. Instead he stood and offered me his hand.

As he pulled me to my feet he said, "What should I bring?"

# # #

"I'm so sorry for your loss." I winced inwardly. It sounded stupid, like you'd misplaced your wallet or something. But that's what people said, right? That they were sorry for someone's loss. I had no idea what else to say.

Dex, Kabita's eldest brother, smiled. Even on the computer screen, I could see the strain around his eyes and the white brackets around his mouth. There was a stain on his blue T-shirt. It looked like he'd been wearing for days. He'd aged ten years since I'd last seen him. Clearly he was grieving heavily. I got it. Kabita and her brothers had always been close, but they'd become closer over the last couple of months or so since their father's death.

"You will come to the service?" He seemed to genuinely want me there.

"Of course," I said. "Just let me know when and where." My smile was a bit strained. I didn't want to sit at some memorial and mourn with a bunch of people who had no idea who Kabita had been. I didn't even want to admit she was gone. I wanted to go out and hunt down the bastards that had hurt her, but I couldn't let her brothers down. They'd been kind to me, and Kabita would want me to go.

I cleared my throat. "Listen, I want to ask you something." How to put this?

"You want to know what she was involved in before she..." He trailed off. Obviously, he didn't want to use that word either. Good. We were in agreement.

"I know you told Trevor you had no idea, but she called me around the time she left London. She, um, wouldn't tell me what she was investigating, only that something was wrong. I wondered if she said something to you? Anything at all."

"Sorry, Morgan, but I told Trevor the truth. She literally disappeared overnight without a word. I have no idea what she was working on at the time. I thought she was just finishing up some final paperwork before returning to Portland." He shrugged, looking a little lost.

"She wasn't acting weird or anything?"

His brow furrowed into deep lines. He was starting to turn silver around the temples. Unfortunately it made him look more like Alister than I was comfortable with. "Actually, now that you mention it, she was behaving strangely. Nothing too obvious, mind you, but she was quieter than usual. More withdrawn. I assumed it was due to everything that's happened over the past few months, coupled with the fact she was returning home to Portland. I attributed it to being homesick. Now I wonder." He rubbed his forehead, his face drawn into a fierce frown.

"Understandable," I assured him, half wishing I could give him a hug though I wasn't exactly a touchy-feely person. "You've all been through so much. I would expect some changes, you know?" I shifted nervously, wanting this call to be over but needing more information. "She left no notes or files?"

"Nothing. I wish I could give you more."

I did, too, but it wouldn't be the first time I'd solved a crime with nothing to go on. And this was my best friend. The woman who'd changed my life. I would hunt the bastard down, and I would make him pay.

Chapter 2

Emory Chastain ran a little herbal shop in the historic district of Sellwood. She also happened to be a portal witch—a rare magic worker who could manipulate the portal systems that crisscrossed our world between this dimension and the next. Lucky for me, because while the portalways could be dangerous, they were a hell of a lot faster than air travel.

Her spell room was at the back of her shop behind a velvet curtain. The walls were deep purple, the ceiling and floor black. A simple shrine to an unfamiliar goddess was tucked into a small alcove on the wall across from the entrance. A metal and glass curio cabinet next to the shrine was filled with the tools of her trade. The center of the floor was bare.

Emory welcomed Inigo and me with a sympathetic smile. Her blue eyes glowed with inner warmth and her strawberry blonde hair shimmered in the dim light of the room. She squeezed my arm as I passed her. "I'm really sorry about Kabita."

I swallowed and muttered, "Thanks." I didn't want sympathy. I wanted revenge. But I couldn't be rude to Emory. She was trying to be kind. Unfortunately, kindness was the last thing I needed right now.

As we gathered in the spell room, Emory paused, her long broomstick skirt swishing around her ankles. "You remember how this works, right?"

Inigo and I nodded. This wouldn't be the first time she'd opened the portals for us.

"It's night in Liverpool, so you should be able to slip in unseen. One of the portals opens in an abandoned warehouse near the waterfront. Look for it."

Inigo and I murmured our understanding. I had no idea how we were supposed to tell one warehouse from a dozen others. Somehow we'd figure it out.

Using a chunk of white chalk, Emory drew several symbols in a wide circle on the floor, as she had many times before. Within the outer circle of symbols, she sketched a single, swirling labyrinth. After returning the chalk to the curio cabinet, she placed white candles on each of the outer symbols, plus a single one in the center of the circle. Then she opened a jar I knew contained salt and poured the white grains around the outside of the circle.

"Remember, don't cross the line of salt until I tell you."

We didn't need to respond. We'd done this often enough. Crossing the salt line meant releasing a lot of powerful and uncontrollable magic into the world. Worse, it could let bad juju into the circle, wreaking havoc with the spell. I so did not want her accidentally summoning a demon because we'd screwed up.

Emory closed her eyes, held her hands above the center candle, and chanted the spell that would open the portalways. The candle sparked, the wick flamed, and I felt the elemental power charging the room. The Darkness within me stirred.

One by one, the candles jumped to life. As the final candle lit, the circle closed.

Emory once again held her hands above it, chanting. The flames leapt higher as her chanting intensified. She uncorked a tiny bottle, waving her palm above it in a circle before swallowing the contents. I knew from experience it was about to get interesting.

The air began to spark and sizzle like a blanket full of static electricity. In the center of the circle, a shimmering orb appeared, floating above Emory's outstretched hands.

I distinctly remembered the first time we'd done this. The damn orb had exploded. I ducked a little, half expecting it to explode again, but Emory seemed to have gotten a handle on the spell. She tossed the orb into the air, where it stretched and twisted until a shimmering portal appeared.

Emory grinned at me. "Come on in."

I stepped into the circle, feeling the usual heady zing along my skin as I passed through the salt line.

Inside the circle, it stank of ozone. Ah, the smell of the portalways.

"Are you sure we'll know the right exit?" I asked, eyeing the portal dubiously.

Emory shrugged. "Believe me, you'll know. The portal you seek is unique. Follow your nose."

I rolled my eyes at her cryptic words, but Inigo gave my hand a reassuring squeeze. I guess he'd know. We stepped through into the shimmering world of the portalways. Ahead stretched tunnels with pearlescent walls dancing with calming colors of blue, green, and purple. In the walls were openings into worlds beyond imagination. I was pretty sure I spotted the pyramids through one of them. Another looked like it might exit into the Otherworld.

I wasn't sure how much time had passed before Inigo grabbed my hand.

"This is it," he said, pausing in front of one of the doorways. I couldn't see anything but blackness.

"Are you sure?"

He snorted. "Of course. I can smell it."

Of course he could. He was half dragon, after all.

Inigo stepped through the portal, and I followed him into utter darkness. After a moment my eyes adjusted, and I could make out the faint trickle of moonlight shining through narrow windows high in the wall. Awkward shapes huddled around us, silent sentinels in the night. I smelled it now, the mustiness and mildew of age and neglect, a slight dampness echoed by the faintest trickle of water, likely from a leaky pipe somewhere nearby. Abandoned? Definitely. The Darkness rose within me, unbidden and unwelcome, just enough to boost my vision. I tried to force it back down — I was still worried about its effect on the peanut — but the Darkness ignored me. The shapes morphed into stacks of rotting pallets and tumbled, empty crates. Cobwebs shimmered in the moonlight, stretched elegantly from rusted machinery and roughhewn beams. This place had been empty for a very long time. No wonder Emory considered it the perfect landing spot for our little foray.

The portal behind us disappeared, leaving us on our own. When we were ready, we'd call Emory, and she'd reopen it for us. Hopefully, in the meantime we could find some clues. I still shied away from the reality that was now my world. I'd become used to Kabita being gone. It made it easier to imagine her still in London and not...

I shook my head and followed Inigo as he wended his way between the pallets and assorted detritus until we reached a door. It was locked from the outside, but a hard yank from my dragon boyfriend snapped the lock. We stepped outside, breathing in the cool, fresh air. Inigo pushed the door shut and pushed the lock so it appeared it was still locked.

"Now what?" he asked, nudging my arm, like a cat butting up against its person. Weird analogy, but it worked. Dragons and cats had a surprising amount in common sometimes.

"Trevor set up a meeting with his contact here in Liverpool. I doubt we'll learn anything new, but it couldn't hurt to hear directly from him."

Inigo nodded. "Lead on."

Since I had zero idea where in the city we were, I used my phone to locate our position. We were somewhere at the edge of the port at three o'clock in the morning. Nowhere near a tube station, even if it was still running at this time of night, and I didn't want to explain to a taxi driver what we were doing here.

"Guess we're walking."

"I could shift," Inigo offered.

I shuddered. "No, thanks." I usually loved flying with him, but lately it made me downright queasy. You'd think the peanut, being a quarter dragon, would like the idea. Not so much.

"It would be a lot faster."

"And messier."

He gave me a quizzical look. Then his expression cleared. "Oh."

"Exactly."

"Nice night for a stroll." His grin was brilliant in the dark as he looped his arm through mine.

We made it to the nearest major street. The warm glow of streetlamps welcomed us to the thoroughfare. Although it was late—or early, depending on how you looked at it—the occasional car zipped by, headed for some unknown destination. It was like we'd stepped back into civilization after too long in the wilderness.

And now I was waxing poetic. Or maudlin. Or something. I stifled a sigh. Too much time thinking. Not good.

My phone chimed with a text from Trevor about the time and location of our meeting: a coffee shop located inside the local library. "We're heading west toward the city center," I said.

"Excellent. I love Liverpool, and it's been years."

I narrowed my eyes. "How many years exactly?"

He had the grace to look embarrassed. "I believe it was about 1886."

"Of course it was."

Let me tell you, it's weird dating a man nearly four centuries older than you. It was easy to forget sometimes. Inigo was into modern culture and technology, unlike many dragonkin who preferred to hang out in the Highlands of Scotland and pretend the rest of the world didn't exist. But every once in a while, he'd say something odd, and I'd remember all those centuries between us, and it would be weird again. Would our kid live for centuries, too? Or would she—or he—have a human lifespan? Apparently it go could either way, depending on how the genes mixed or something.

Distracting myself with inane mental ramblings would only work so long. What I needed to do was to focus on the mission.

We'd been walking for nearly an hour on cobbled streets past Victorian brick buildings when I gave in to the hunger pangs. Eating these days was iffy. I was hungry, but I hated puking and puking seemed like a regular thing. So much fun.

I dug around in my satchel and pulled out a granola bar, munching on it as we walked. Chocolate chip, naturally. I hesitated after two bites. I frowned at the snack. Could pregnant women eat chocolate? Was it safe for the peanut?

"It's dogs," Inigo said. His glasses caught the streetlight and reflected it back.

I stared at him, confused. "What?"

"Dogs can't eat chocolate. You're fine."

Oh. "Are you reading my mind again?"

"Hard not to. You're practically screaming at me." His tone was dry, but his expression was full of adoration.

I frowned. Great. Now he'd know for sure what a crazed lunatic I'd become. "It's the damn hormones," I said lamely.

He wisely said nothing. He waved down a passing taxi, the light on the roof glowing bright yellow in the night.

The taxi stank of stale cigarette smoke—which was totally illegal, by the way—and human sweat not quite overpowered by a musky cologne. To say it was unpleasant was an understatement. My stomach turned dangerously, and I stuffed the rest of the granola bar back in my bag.

Fortunately the car ride took about ten minutes. A minute longer, and the driver would have had to detail his car.

We stood on a cobbled footpath in front of the rotunda of Central Library. The entire street was dark, the shops closed up tight. The sky was just turning gray as dawn hovered on the horizon. I peered at the sign out front.

"It doesn't open until nine," I groused. "What are we supposed to do until then?"

"They should be opening soon," Inigo said, pointing down the street to a bakery. I could smell the perfume of fresh-baked bread and, surprisingly, it didn't make me want to hurl. We walked slowly, trying to kill time.

A woman in a white apron appeared out front, propping up an A-frame sign listing the daily specials. Even though it was still ten minutes until opening, she waved us over and urged us to sit inside the fragrant warmth of the bakery. We ordered coffee—decaf for me—the waiter gave me a funny look but complied— and regular for Inigo, as well as croissants with jam. Very continental. What wasn't continental was the ham and eggs we also ordered. Vampire hunting required protein.

We took our time, practically drowning ourselves in coffee before finally ambling over to the library, where we found an empty bench to people watch. At nine a.m. on the dot, a slender man in a three-piece suit and wearing round spectacles sidled up to us and sat down without so much as a good morning. I gave him a look. He didn't quail. I guessed he was made of sterner stuff than one might think.

"Nice day for a picnic," he said in a Liverpuddlian accent.

I resisted a sigh of exasperation. Trevor and his spy games. "Hope there aren't any ants," I chirped.

"Ah, then it is you." He appeared pleased, although he didn't so much as crack a smile.

"If you say so."

"Phillip Mortimer. Trevor sent me. I work for the agency." I could only assume he meant MI8. Inigo and I introduced ourselves and shook hands. All very proper.

"What have you got for us?" It came out a little blunter than I meant it to, but I was getting antsy.

"Are you sure you want to see these?" Mortimer asked, pulling a file from his briefcase. "They aren't terribly pleasant."

I held out my hand. He gave me the file, albeit reluctantly. I laid it on my lap and opened it. My breakfast tried to break free and run.

Inside were pictures of Kabita's body and the muddy bank where they'd pulled her from the river. It almost looked like she was sleeping, except she was soaked through, and her skin had a bluish cast, as if she had been drained of blood.

I cleared my throat. "No bite marks?"

Mortimer's expression was one of sympathy. "None."

Inigo studied the photos carefully. "No forensic evidence whatsoever?"

"None at all. According to our experts, she was, er, she entered the water somewhere north of here a few hours before she was discovered. The coroner has been unable to establish cause of death." He said it almost apologetically.

"So, it wasn't drowning," I said, not sure if I was relieved or not.

"No. It wasn't. No water in the lungs." He cleared his throat. "It is most unfortunate, losing such a great hunter."

Kabita had not only been an extraordinarily talented demon hunter, she'd been my trainer, and there had been others before me. She'd been good at what she did, although there'd been times I'd wanted to punch her in the face. Now I wished I could take back every angry thought I'd had during training. I wanted my friend back.

"Where is she?" I asked, my voice a little strangled. I wanted to see her and I didn't at the same time. If I saw her—her body—maybe I could accept she was gone. But if I didn't, I could live in denial a little while longer.

"She has been returned to London. To her family." His voice was gentle.

"Of course," I murmured, oddly relieved. Denial it was. "You have no idea why she was in Liverpool?" I couldn't seem to take my eyes off the photo.

"I am sorry, but no. She did not check in with the local field office, and none of her usual contacts were aware she was even in the city."

Inigo reached over and shut the folder. I breathed a sigh of relief.

"Anything else you can give us?" he asked Phillip.

"Perhaps. One small thing. It may be nothing, but it may be something. There is a young woman in town. She has been showing up at various places during the investigation, following my men. She's surprisingly adept at the spy game for one so young. We have yet to determine who she is." He pulled his phone from his pocket and showed me the screen. I sucked in a breath. He gave me a penetrating glance. "You know her then?"

I nodded. "Jade. Jade Vincent. What's she doing here?"

Phillip frowned. "Jade?"

I smiled grimly. "The last dragon hunter."

Chapter 3

"I thought we wiped her memory," Inigo muttered as we hurried down the street after parting ways with Mortimer. The sun was up and cast the narrow streets in long shadows. Gargoyles peered at us from corners, and I wondered if they were ordinary manmade statues or if they were like the real life gargoyles that protected Prague. It was hard to tell.

"We did," I assured him. "Completely. She should have no memory of you, me, Kabita, or the things she and Alister did. She should have no idea that dragons are real, never mind that she's a hunter."

Jade had once been under the mind control of the evil Queen of the Sidhe and Kabita's psycho father, Alister Jones, and I'm not talking a little brainwashing. Morgana, the Sidhe Queen, quite literally stuck her fingers in Jade's brain and manipulated her mind. They'd amplified the natural crazy that was the nature of dragon hunters in order to use her against me and my friends. They'd very nearly succeeded. Instead, Alister and Morgana were dead, and we were able to erase Jade's memories and return her to her home in London, none the wiser. It had been safest for all concerned, including Jade.

Now she was back. What that meant was anyone's guess, but I couldn't imagine it involved puppies and unicorns.

I glanced at the paper Phillip Mortimer had given me. The address written on it was a few streets over near the Cavern Club, where the Beatles had once played. It was still ridiculously early for a house call, but I wasn't about to wait.

Jade Vincent lived in a fifth-floor walkup off Victoria Street on Temple Lane, which meant I had to hike my pregnant ass up five flights of very steep stairs in a stairwell that stank of musty old brick mixed with boiled Brussels sprouts. Why on earth anybody sane would boil Brussels sprouts was beyond me. I was more than a little queasy by the time we reached the red door marked with a brass #5-2. Across the hall was #5-1. I guessed there were only two flats per floor in this building.

The door swung open before either of us had a chance to knock. On the other side stood a petite, platinum blonde, pixie-like girl no more than twenty-two with the brashness to match. Her T-shirt was black with white letters that read **I hope you step on a Lego**. I hid a grin. Nice.

"About time you got here." Jade stepped back as if she expected us to come inside. So we did, albeit with some confusion and a whole lot of caution. The last time we'd seen Jade, she hadn't exactly been a fan of me or Inigo. The fact that she not only remembered but expected us was cause for concern.

"Excuse me?" I said as I stepped into her tiny front room. The only furniture was a beanbag chair and a small television set about twenty years out of date. I didn't know what else to say or do, so I stood there, staring at her, Inigo firmly stuck to my side.

She let out a huff of breath and rolled her eyes at the same time. "It's okay, you know. I remember. Well, sort of. I remember you for sure." She nodded at me. Well, that didn't bode well.

Inigo eyed her. "How is that possible?"

"You mean because you guys wiped my brain?" She gave us a wicked grin.

I gave a huff of exasperation. "Don't be ridiculous. We didn't wipe your brain. We removed some of the more...difficult memories." And technically I had nothing to do with it, but I doubted she'd appreciate the semantics.

"Yeah, well it didn't work. Not entirely, anyway. Coffee?" She clomped across the postage stamp-sized living room to an even smaller kitchen area. I joined her, leaning one hip against the canary yellow counter. Inigo remained in the doorway. Wasn't much room for him in the kitchen.

"Only if you have decaf," I said.

Jade lifted a brow, then she sniffed the air like a damn dog. "Oh my god," she squealed, practically jumping up and down like she'd won the freaking lottery. "You're preggers." Her British accent was especially thick all of a sudden. I wasn't about to ask how she knew. She was a hunter, not a dragon, so she shouldn't have been able to smell anything. All I knew was I was damn tired of people sniffing me.

"Um, yeah." What else was there to say?

"Sorry, no decaf, but I've got herbal tea."

"I'll stick with water, thanks."

She shrugged as if to say "suit yourself" and handed me a glass of water before fiddling with a stovetop cappuccino machine. "Well, it's exciting. Do you know what it is yet?"

"A baby."

She gave me an annoyed look. "Boy or girl."

"No idea."

"Not to interrupt this bonding moment, but I think you need to explain this memory thing," Inigo said dryly.

"Oh, right." Jade turned the knob for the gas burner, then crossed her arms and stared at the ceiling for a moment as if collecting said memories. "I was in London, right? Everything was fine. Job was going well. Started seeing this totally hot chick, Louisa." She fanned herself. "Oo-la-la. Then one day I'm on the Tube, and there's this guy, and I know he's not human, right?"

"Sure," I agreed, still confused.

Inigo's eyes narrowed. "How?"

"No clue." The cappuccino thingy started steaming. She turned to pour herself and Inigo cups of coffee. "It was like I could smell him. Not with my nose, exactly, but like with something else. It's weird. Anyway, I followed him. No idea why. Just impulse, I guess. He went into this alley and *bam!*" I nearly jumped at her yell. "He got me. I swear I thought he was going to beat me up or something, but instead he looked really surprised and called me hunter, and I'm like 'what's that?' Next thing I know, we're in a coffee shop and he's telling me about dragons and shit."

Inigo and I stared at her in something like shock. Finally I cleared my throat. "And you believed him?"

"Hard not to when he shifted right in front of me. Talk about gobsmacked." She sipped her coffee calmly.

"Did this guy have a name?" I asked.

"Yeah. Drago something?"

Inigo pinched the bridge of his nose as if in pain. "I need to have a talk with that brother of mine."

"He's your brother? Sweet!"

"What happened after you talked to Drago?" I asked, ignoring her outburst, although I totally agreed with Inigo. Drago, of all people, knew why we'd removed Jade's memories. Dragon hunters had always been an unstable lot. Probably why Jade was the last one in existence. Keeping her away from dragons was the best way to keep her sane and the rest of us out of danger. From her, at least.

33

"He told me about dragon hunters and how our job was to hunt rogue dragons and shit. So cool. Then he offered to train me."

"What?" Inigo all but roared.

"Cool, right?" She beamed as if it was the best thing ever. Maybe for her it was. She seemed more stable than I'd ever seen her, so whatever Drago was doing, it appeared to be working.

"So he trained you?" I prompted.

"Yeah. Started meeting up a couple times a week. Lot of hand-to-hand, weapons stuff. Whatever. It was fun, and it felt good to be doing something physical. I started having these weird dreams about living in the States and fighting with these people and doing some pretty crazy shit, so I asked Drago about it, and he explained." She sobered. "I am sorry, you know. I really am."

"We know," Inigo assured her. "It wasn't your fault. You'd been manipulated."

She frowned fiercely, her cheeks turning an angry red. "Yeah. That Alister Jones would have a lot to answer for if he weren't dead already." She seemed to mentally brush it off, perking up again. "I started to realize I had a lot to make up for, so I kept training with Drago."

"How'd you end up in Liverpool?" I asked, not ready yet to give up my distrust of her. I knew what had happened wasn't her fault. She hadn't been in control of her actions. Still, it was hard to let go of it.

"Drago got word of a dragon gone rogue here, so he sent me with one of his lieutenants to hunt the thing."

"And did you?" Inigo asked.

"Sure. For a week now. But that's the weird thing." She frowned, sipping her coffee again. Inigo's cup sat on the counter, its contents growing cold.

"What is?" we asked in unison.

"A whole week hunting, and you'd think I'd have found some trace of the thing, right? But there isn't a trace anywhere of a rogue dragon."

"Then why would Drago send you here?" I asked, wondering if he'd done it to get the sassy kid out of his hair.

"I said there wasn't a sign of a rogue," she said with a quirk of her lips. "But there's plenty of signs someone's trying to *make* it look like there's a rogue."

Inigo frowned. "You mean—"

"I mean, there isn't a rogue dragon in Liverpool, but someone sure wants people to think there is."

Chapter 4

"Do you think this fake rogue is the reason Kabita came to Liverpool?" Inigo asked, slouching down beside me on the floor next to Jade's beanbag chair, where I perched.

"Kabita's in Liverpool?" Jade asked. "Since when?"

I gave her a look. "You remember her, too?"

"Not really. Just what Drago told me. I had no idea she was here. Maybe she can help."

Inigo glanced at me. "I doubt it. She's dead."

Jade's mouth hung open. Her shock was obvious and unfeigned as far as I could tell. She sank down to sit cross-legged on the floor. "Damn. What happened?"

"We don't know. She was found in the Mersey two days ago. No sign of how she died or who killed her, if anyone." Inigo sounded calm, but I could feel the tension thrumming in him. I placed my palm on his back to calm him. It seemed to work.

Jade propped her chin on her hand and tapped her cheek thoughtfully. "Kabita was a demon hunter, right?"

I stared at her for a beat, wondering what her angle was. "Yeah. Why?"

"You really think she died for no reason? I don't think so." Jade snorted derisively. "I'm betting there's something supernatural involved here. I have an idea. Why don't you let me track her?"

"She's not a dragon," I said dryly.

Jade shrugged. "Tracking is tracking. I can track a dragon, I can track a demon hunter. Maybe it'll help us figure out what happened."

I leaned forward, staring at her intently, waiting for the evil I'd once seen to show. It wasn't there no matter how hard I looked. "Why do you want to help so much?"

She sighed, scrubbing her hand through her short hair. "I have a lot to make up for, you know? I don't remember it, but it happened. I need to prove, to myself if no one else, I'm not that person anymore."

I exchanged glances with Inigo. He nodded subtly. We could use all the help we could get.

"Okay," I agreed. "Where do we start?"

"Where I always start on a hunt," Jade said with a grin. "Down at the pub."

# # #

Pretty much every city in the world had an Irish pub. It's like a rule or something. Liverpool was known for its large Irish population, so I wasn't terribly surprised when Jade stopped halfway down Mathew Street in front of a white brick building with a large green-and-white sign that read **O'Leary's**. Out front waved the green, white, and orange Irish flag. A blackboard A-frame sign out front read **Soup of the day: beer**. If I hadn't been so focused on the task at hand, I might have been amused.

The inside of the pub looked pretty much like every other traditional Irish pub the world over. The floors were plank and scuffed, the bar wood and polished, the music Celtic and loud. Taps lined one end of the counter and bottles crammed the back shelves. It was late morning, and the bar had just opened, but a couple of what were likely regulars huddled in corner booths. I smelled food cooking somewhere in the back. Something meaty and starchy. I wasn't sure if it smelled good or I wanted to puke again.

The bartender glanced up as we entered, a broad smile creasing his freckled face. "Well, if it isn't Ms. Jade Vincent. How you doin', love?" His accent was a blend of Liverpuddlian and Irish. He was beefy and brawny, and I wouldn't have wanted to meet him in a dark alley.

"Not too bad, thanks," Jade said with a grin. "You're looking fine, Collin." She winked at him saucily.

His cheeks turned as red as his hair. "Go on with you now."

"Morgan, Inigo, I'd like you to meet my friend, Collin."

Collin's eyes widened. "*The* Morgan?"

Jade nodded. "The one and only."

"'Tis an honor to be sure." He grabbed my hand and shook with unbridled enthusiasm, his accent getting more Irish by the minute.

"Uh, right. Likewise."

He snorted. "I'm nobody. But you. You're..." He glanced around, then leaned forward and said in a low voice, "You're a *hunter.*"

I glanced at Jade, who nodded. "He knows."

"Is he——?"

"Just a plain old boring human," Collin interrupted. "Although there was a hunter in my family in the distant past. Very distant. That's why I love hearing Jade's stories. Any friend of hers is a friend of mine."

I didn't bother telling him that calling Jade a friend was a stretch of epic proportions. "I take it Collin is your contact."

"Oh, I wish," Collin said with a snort. "Afraid you supernaturals look down on us lowly ordinary folk." He glanced at Jade. "He'll be here soon enough. What's your poison?"

"It's a little early in the morning for drinking, don't you think?" Jade asked with a lifted eyebrow.

"Depends on who you ask."

"Just give me an orange juice," she said.

Inigo ordered a cola. I stuck with ginger ale. No sense poking the bear, so to speak.

Several minutes passed awkwardly as we sat in silence, sipping our drinks. Finally a shadow blocked the sunlight streaming through the open door of the pub.

"He's here," Jade said softly without even looking. She set her bottle of orange juice on the bar. "Follow me."

We left our drinks and followed her past the bar and up a set of stairs. At the top we turned left into a small room set up with a single long table. One of those rentable party rooms, no doubt. At the moment it was empty, though the heavy curtains were pulled back to admit as much sunlight as possible, which wasn't much.

A couple minutes later, in walked a very large, very scary looking man. His hair was the color of fire, the bright orange-red part on the far edge of the flame, as was the day old scruff of whiskers on his chin. His eyes were an eerie gold speckled with green. He wore full-on Highland dress, from the plaid tossed over his shoulder to the matching kilt, like he was an extra from *Outlander*. His energy was, well, definitely not human.

"Hunter." It came out as a growl, and I wasn't sure if he was talking to Jade or me.

Jade nodded. "Vane."

Inigo had gone still, his eyes shifting from his usual blue to bright gold. His dragon was close to the surface. I opened my mouth to question him, but Vane spoke first, bowing slightly as he did so.

"Your Highness."

He knew who Inigo was?

Vane turned to me and bowed again. "Blessed be the mother of the dragon kin."

That was a first. "Um, excuse me?"

"Vane is dragon kin," Inigo said, eyes still on the newcomer. "He can sense the presence of another one of our kind." He meant the peanut. Holy shit.

"Okay. Thanks, I think?"

A slight smile quirked Vane's lips, which didn't make him look any less scary. "You're welcome."

"Who are you exactly?" I demanded.

"It's complicated."

"Give it a try." I gave him a "don't fuck with me" look.

His lips quirked again. So I amused him, did I? Well, we'd see about that. I tapped my foot impatiently.

"You might refer to me as the king's assassin," Vane said.

I glanced at Inigo. "Your brother has a personal assassin?"

Inigo shifted uncomfortably. "Drago is the dragon king, after all."

"Still. Most kings these days don't have assassins running around."

"No. These days they call them spies," Jade said dryly.

Good point. "Okay, fine. Who exactly do you run around killing?" I asked Vane.

"Whoever is in need of it."

I stared at him.

He chuckled. "Those that threaten the dragon kin."

"Like rogue dragons?" I guessed.

He nodded. "Sometimes, though dragon hunters are usually better at that sort of thing. Sometimes we work together."

"What do you know about Kabita? Was she here hunting a rogue?"

"I met with her shortly after she arrived in Liverpool and, yes, she had a theory there was a rogue on the loose. At least initially."

I sank into one of the chairs at the long table. "Tell me."

He sat down across from me and propped his elbows on the table. "Over the last few weeks, a number of bodies have been found. Vagrants mostly. Panhandlers and thieves. The sorts of people no one would miss. They were all found bloodless and with deep marks in their bodies not unlike those caused by claws."

I frowned. It sounded like a cross between vampire and dragon. Or shifter, maybe. "Go on."

He leaned back, the chair creaking under his massive weight. "Kabita was convinced there was a rogue. I was not. Although she listened to my argument, we agreed to disagree and went our separate ways. Unfortunately, that was the last I saw of Kabita Jones."

"Do you know where she was staying?" I asked.

He shook his head regretfully. "I am sorry. I do not."

I sighed. "If not a rogue, what do you think is killing these people?"

He gave me a long look. "I believe there is something else at work here. Something very dark and very evil."

"Wow. Lotta help there, Vane."

He shrugged. "It's what I've got."

"Why would this dark and evil thing want to make it look like there's a rogue dragon on the loose? What would be the point?"

"You've got me." He stood to leave but paused a moment, eyes snaring mine. "Watch your back, hunter." And with that cryptic warning, he was gone.

Chapter 5

"How'd it go?" Haakon Magnussen glanced up from the stack of paperwork in front of him. The big, blond, Viking Sunwalker looked out of place behind Kabita's desk, even if it was a massive mahogany thing. He'd done a good job taking over for her while she was in London, though. I wondered vaguely if he'd be taking over permanently now.

I'd managed to catch a nap after we returned to Portland, but I wanted to catch Haakon up as quickly as possible. Exhaustion weighed heavily on me, and I sighed as I sank into one of the visitor's chairs and laid my head back. "This kid is wearing me out."

He lifted an eyebrow. "Imagine your exhaustion when he or she is out running about."

"Gee, thanks," I said, not bothering to raise my head.

He gave me a long look. "You didn't answer my question."

I closed my eyes. "I know."

"I'm sorry about Kabita."

"I know that, too."

He sighed. "I hadn't heard from her in days. Before she..." he trailed off. I guess he wasn't comfortable with using the "D" word either. That, or he just wasn't comfortable using it around me.

"Neither had I," I admitted, finally lifting my head. "I wish she'd let me know what was going on so I could help her." But that was Kabita for you. Stoic to a fault.

"Tell me about Liverpool."

I told him what we'd learned from Jade and Vane, about Kabita suspecting a rogue dragon on the loose but Vane believing that it was something darker.

"What can possibly be worse than a rogue dragon?" Haakon asked with a frown. The sun streaming through the window turned his blond hair bright gold. It reminded me of dragon eyes.

"You got me. Jade didn't know either. I've got a call in to Eddie. Hopefully he can help." Eddie Mulligan was not only my friend and a living encyclopedia of all things supernatural, he was also an immortal Titan, which was both cool and scary if you thought about it. "Until I hear from him, I'm at your disposal."

"You sure you can still do this?" he asked bluntly.

I narrowed my eyes. "Do what? My job?"

"Don't get snippy." He glared at me with Viking badassery, which I ignored.

"Don't get smug and superior, or you'll find a blade at your throat."

He didn't even bat an eyelash. Damned Viking bastard. "Very well. But I'm worried about you and the child."

"The child is fine. It's the size of a plum. It doesn't do much but hang around and make me irritable."

"We don't know what a vampire bite might do to it."

I rolled my eyes. "A vampire isn't going to bite the peanut. It's going to bite me, and since I've already been exposed to the virus and am immune, I think we're good. Besides, the kid is a quarter dragon." Dragons couldn't be turned. Something about their physiology killed the vampire virus, like bleach killing common cold germs.

"Still."

"Still nothing," I snapped. "Lots of women work when pregnant. This is the twenty-first century, Haakon, not the Dark Ages."

"Medieval. I'm only a thousand years old."

"Whatever."

He sighed. "Most women don't hunt vampires or slay demons for a living."

He had a point, but what did he expect me to do? Lay around eating bonbons? I had a murder to solve. Besides, now that Kabita was gone, I was the only hunter in Portland.

"What does the father think about it?"

I all but growled. "The *father* has enough sense to keep his opinions to himself." Which wasn't totally fair. Inigo had been completely supportive. Was he nervous about me kicking vampire ass while pregnant with his child? Sure, but he knew I could handle myself and trusted me not to behave like a total idiot.

Haakon shrugged. "If you think you can do the job, that's good enough for me."

I wasn't sure whether to be irritated or relieved. He wasn't my boss. He was sort of a friend, I supposed. He sometimes helped me on a hunt, and I'd trusted him with my life on more than one occasion. It was a weird relationship.

"You're still in charge?" I asked.

He shrugged. "For the time being. The SRA doesn't want to leave a vacuum."

"Makes sense." I certainly didn't want to be in charge.

"I guess that means you're up to dispatching a demon," Haakon said, switching topics.

I grimaced. Demons were Kabita's purview. *Had* been anyway. I had helped when she needed it, but I'd take a vamp over the denizens of the Hel Realm any day. However, with Kabita gone, it was all hands on deck. Even though what I wanted to do was track her killer, I'd hit a dead end. Nothing to track, so demon hunting it was.

"Sure." I dropped my booted feet to the floor with a thump. "What have you got?"

Haakon tapped a few keys on his laptop. "Sending the file to you now. We're dealing with a Nybbas demon."

"Not familiar with that one."

"Pretty typical demonic fare: cloven hooves, horns, and whatnot."

I opened the file on my smartphone to find an old timey drawing of the classic devil, dressed in a fancy outfit and wearing a whole lot of jewelry. "Powers?"

"Visions."

"Shit."

"No kidding. According to what I've read, once they've got their psychic hooks in, you're toast. They can conjure up anything they want, and as far as you're concerned, that's reality. I read a story of a guy who walked off the roof of a building because he thought he was walking into an elevator."

"That doesn't sound good."

"It wasn't," he said. "The building was twenty stories high."

Definitely not good. "Weaknesses?"

"They're not taken very seriously in the Hel Realms. In fact, I believe they're mocked quite thoroughly. So, I'm guessing ego."

"Got it covered. How do you kill them?"

"You don't. They're surprisingly powerful, though rare. Banishing them back to Hel is the best you can hope for."

Goody. And I was fresh out of holy water. "Where was this thing last seen?"

"Southwest, out near Multnomah Village. Woman claims her eight-year-old son nearly walked into traffic. She grabbed him before he could come to any harm, but he kept insisting they were at Disneyland, and he wanted to get on the teacups or some shit."

"Jesus."

"I don't think the Jew has anything to do with this." He was totally serious.

I snorted. "Very funny." I stood, feeling a little woozy as I did so. I'd lost my most recent meal. What I needed was a donut. "I'm on it. I'll get back to you."

Chapter 6

The beautiful thing about Portland is that there are so many donut places to choose from. Sure, Voodoo is famous all over the country. Those pink boxes have a downright Pavlovian effect, but honestly? I know some places that would blow your mind.

Blue Box Donut Shoppe may have been a touch out of the way, but desperate times. I swung through downtown and parked across the block. There was a short line, but it moved quickly, and I was soon double-fisting a raspberry pistachio and a double chocolate salted caramel. Ah, bliss.

I think the peanut liked donuts, too, because by the time I finished them, I was feeling all kinds of better. Time to kick some demonic ass.

Multnomah Village was pretty much what it said on the tin: a lovely little village in Multnomah County. Tucked into a corner of Southwest Portland, it's been fairly untouched by the ravages of rent hikes, hipsters, and overcrowding.

I parked in the middle of the village, across the street from Annie Bloom's Bookstore, where the demon had last been seen. Or rather, the effects of the demon had been seen. Apparently no one had actually seen the Nybbas. Not unusual. Human minds have a way of glossing over what they can't—or won't—understand, and from what I could tell, a Nybbas could easily cloud someone's mind to forget he or she had ever seen the thing.

My hunter senses, which worked brilliantly on vampires, weren't exactly stellar when it came to demons. No more than what any ordinary human might feel in the presence of evil. Tracking the thing was going to be a bitch. I had no way of knowing if it had moved on or what. There had been no further reports of near-death experiences or random confusion. According to what I'd read in the file, Nybbas demons liked to stay close to a particular area. Sort of sink in and put down roots, if you will. Trick was finding the bastard. Short of whistling for it like a dog, I'd have to basically luck onto it. Not my preferred method of hunting. Usually when I went demon hunting, I had Kabita to help me.

My stomach dropped as I remembered I was never going to have her help again. I shoved that thought aside. I did not need to be dwelling on it right now.

Multnomah Village was set on the side of a small hill with Capitol Highway running right through the middle of downtown. Not that it looked like a highway at that point. Just two narrow lanes with parking on either side of the street and stop signs every couple of blocks. Shops and cafes lined the

highway, and pedestrians enjoyed the wide sidewalks
and afternoon sunshine.

I walked slowly up one side of the street past gift,
candy, and pie shops and down the other. Nothing.
As I passed Renner's, a dive bar with excellent food
and beverages and a laid-back atmosphere. Cheerful
reggae music played over the outside speakers. I came
to a halt in front of a narrow alleyway that ran
between Renner's and the dry cleaners next door.
Barely wide enough to allow a single person to pass, it
led to a set of concrete steps that then ascended to
Troy Street, which ran behind Renner's and the other
shops on the north side of the highway.

A chill drifted from the alley. Not the normal
chill one would expect to feel in a shaded spot, but
something darker, harder, scarier.

"Well, well," I muttered, toying with the hilt of
my dagger. "What have we got here?"

I slipped a small aerosol can out of my hip
pocket. It looked like any ordinary can of pepper
spray, but it was salt-infused holy water. The thing
about vampires and holy water? That's a myth, but
demons? It'll melt that shit like acid.

"Here, little Nyggas," I called softly as I entered
the alleyway. "Come to Mama."

I swear the alley grew colder as I repressed a
shiver. I heard a chittering sound, but I didn't see
anything. The alley was empty. I remembered
Haakon's warning. The Nyggas messed with your

mind, which meant the creature could be standing right in front of me, and I wouldn't see it.

I took another step forward, and it was like my feet were suddenly mired in molasses. I tried raising a foot, but it was stuck in the morass. I couldn't move. Panic set in. My heart pounded wildly in my chest as I struggled to breathe. The Darkness went batshit.

It billowed out of me, shrieking like an angry schoolgirl, as vampires rushed in from every side. I jerked my dagger from its sheath and swung wildly at one of them. It went right through the vamp like the creature was made of thin air, but the vamp's teeth sank into my forearm like the real deal. Blood spurted from my arm, and pain lanced up my shoulder. My knees buckled.

I lashed out again with my blade and the Darkness, but it made zero impact on the vamps. A second vamp latched onto my shoulder with its fangs. The pain swamped me. I tumbled to my knees, taking both vamps with me. I stabbed at them again and again, to no avail. I couldn't kill them. They were going to kill me.

Then my brain reengaged. "They're not real," I whispered. "They're not real. Concentrate on what's real." I said it over and over, like a mantra. The pain receded, and I managed to stagger to my feet. I began to chant, not in English, but in an arcane language known only to the witchblood. Fortunately, I'd picked it up as I went along.

I held the little can of holy water in front of me
and sprayed. There was an unholy scream that chilled
me to my marrow. The vamps disappeared. I sprayed
again and made out the outline of the Nyggas demon.
I sprayed and sprayed, chanting as I did so. It was a
spell I'd heard Kabita chant a thousand times when
fighting demons. I didn't understand the words, but I
knew it was a banishing spell meant to open the gates
of Hel, so to speak.

A portal appeared in midair, a spiraling red-orb
thing. Hot, dry wind whipped around me, tossing my
hair wildly in every direction as the portal sucked
everything toward it. An old beer can, worn and
flattened, zipped through the air, whizzing past my
head. It disappeared into the portal. The energy of the
portal plucked at me, urging me to enter. I planted a
palm against the cool brick wall of Renner's and
ignored the call, grounding myself in my own
dimension. I had no intention of spending the rest of
my life in Hel.

I chanted and sprayed until my throat was raw
and my voice cracked. My hand cramped, and the
bottle ran out of holy water. Then, with a final
scream, the demon was sucked through the portal and
the orb snapped shut. Everything went still and quiet.
I let out a shaky breath and leaned against the brick
wall with relief. That had been a little more intense
than I'd bargained for.

"Miss? You okay?"

I turned to find one of the Renner's wait staff standing behind me, a worried look on his chubby face. His black apron was smudged with grease, and his round hipster glasses were half steamed up. He had one of those weird Amish-looking beards that just look dumb unless worn by an actual Amish person.

I stared at him for a moment, confused. "What?"

"I heard a scream."

Damn. He'd heard the demon. "Oh, that was nothing." I gave him an awkward smile. "I just stubbed my toe. Kinda dangerous back here." I did a little hop thing to prove it.

He gave me a look that spoke volumes about my perceived lack of intelligence before ambling back inside. The scent of cooking hamburgers wafted my way as the door swung shut behind him. My stomach both revolted and rumbled in hunger. Damn, I wished it would make up its mind.

Exhausted to the very bone, I dragged myself back to the car. What I wanted was a nap. What I was going to do was continue my investigation. Kabita's murderer would not go unpunished. Not if I had anything to say about it.

Chapter 7

Taking a shower immediately after a demon killing is a smart idea. Things tend to get icky with demons. Slime, pus, various other grossness.

With fatigue pressing down on me, I took the quickest shower I could manage. I wanted to keep going, find Kabita's killer, but my body had other ideas. Naptime was next on the agenda whether I liked it or not.

Hair still wet, I wrapped myself in my ugly, fuzzy pink robe and padded to the bedroom. My bed had never looked so soft and fluffy or inviting. I climbed in, robe and all, and was asleep before my head hit the pillow.

At first I floated on a warm bed of darkness. It was calm, peaceful, happy. I smiled as my muscles unwound and my body relaxed. For the first time in what felt like weeks, I didn't feel like puking. Ah, this must be nirvana.

Then, out of the darkness, an image appeared. Dim and blurry at first, it eventually clarified until I could make it out.

"Kabita?" I reached out, but my hand passed through her like she wasn't there.

Her face was twisted into a scary semblance of herself. She looked… angry. Maybe because her murder hadn't been solved?

"I'm working on it," I assured her. "I promise I'm going to find out who did this."

She didn't say anything, just gazed at me with that scary expression. She clutched something in her hand. I couldn't make it out, but it seemed to frustrate her. She turned and walked away. Before she disappeared into the ether, she let out a shriek of anger and frustration that scared me half to death.

I sat bolt upright, blade already in hand. It was an automatic thing. The reaction of a hunter.

Except the shrieking wasn't a ghost. It was my blasted doorbell.

I staggered into the living room. I must have looked a fright as I threw open the door, but the scrawny dude with the bad Beatles haircut didn't even blink. He couldn't have been more than twenty-two. He gave me a sunny smile.

"Hi, there!" His voice was far too cheerful for any time of day. I noticed he was holding a couple bottles of those snake-oil cleaning products that promise the moon and stars only to relieve you of your hard-earned money without doing a damned thing.

"You selling something?" I snapped. "I'm not interested."

"Wait!"

I closed the door in his face with a smug smile of satisfaction. There was little I found more irritating than door-to-door salesmen who wouldn't take "no" for an answer.

He shouted from the other side of the door. "You dirty ass whore!"

That tore it. I ripped open the door, stomped outside in nothing but my bathrobe and bare feet, and glared at the little pissant. "What did you say?"

He blanched a little, but stuck his lower jaw out mulishly. "Fucking rude bitch." Actually, he didn't say "bitch" but something far ruder.

I punched him in the face.

He flew back and landed on his ass in the neighbor's yard. "Better watch your back, douchebag. Next time think twice before behaving like a misogynistic jackass." I stomped inside without so much as a backward glance.

I slammed the front door, locked it, and turned only to stop dead. A man sat on my couch, blond hair tucked neatly back in a queue. His leather leggings and tunic were deceptively simple, but the sword at his side whispered of magic. He gazed at me with eerie, silver eyes, a slight smile curving his perfect lips.

"What the fuck, Kalen?"

He grinned. "And a good afternoon to you, as well, Hunter. Nicely done by the way."

I snorted. Like I needed his praise. The kid had been a hundred pounds soaking wet. He'd just needed a lesson in not being a sexist asshole. "What are you doing in my living room? I didn't know the Fairy King made house calls."

He grimaced. The Sidhe didn't much like being called fairies. I couldn't blame them. It would be like calling a piranha a goldfish. Same species, whole different character.

"I apologize for the awkwardness of this meeting." He shifted slightly, and one of my fluffy pillows tumbled to the floor. "But it was necessary."

"Was it?" I picked up the pillow and set it carefully on the couch. It was a ridiculous thing, but it had been a gift from Kabita. She'd thought the place needed sprucing up.

"It was also necessary to keep it a secret."

I sighed and scrubbed my eyes. They felt like sandpaper. My nap had been less than refreshing, and after dealing with the salesman douchenozzle, I was not at my best. "All right. I'll bite."

"I need you in the Otherworld."

"Don't tell me a vamp got loose in fairyland."

"I wish it were that simple. No, it is something else. Something more... sinister."

"Can't it wait? I was *trying* to take a nap."

His expression was grim. "There is no time for napping, Morgan. My people are sick. They're dying."

I blinked. "What? The Sidhe? How is that even possible?" The Sidhe didn't get sick, and they certainly didn't die from illness. In fact, they were about as

close to immortal as you could get. They lived for
thousands, sometimes millions of years, most of them
dying of unnatural means.

"I'm afraid it is so."

"Listen, I don't know what you expect me to do
about some kind of Sidhe flu, but—"

"This is far worse than a case of the sniffles,
believe me. I wouldn't be here unless I needed your
help."

"Gee. Way to make a girl feel appreciated."

He grimaced. "You know what I mean. Having a
hunter in their midst is not entirely comfortable for
the Sidhe, particularly one who was responsible for
the death of their queen."

"Bitch deserved it, and you know it." In fact,
he'd helped with her death in a roundabout way.

"Be that as it may, knowing a human can kill one
of us is a distressing thought." He didn't sound
distressed, but then Kalen had his own way of looking
at the world that was odd even for a Sidhe.

"Yeah, I can see how that would be
problematic," I said dryly.

"I need your help. Will you come?"

I heaved an exasperated sigh and stomped to my
bedroom, Kalen on my heels. "Why not? I'm not
going to sleep now anyway."

"Your enthusiasm is noted," he said, following
me into my bedroom.

"Good. Now shut up and get out of here so I can dress." No way was I entering the Otherworld in my robe and nothing else.

He gave an elegant bow. "As you wish." He blinked out of existence. Not really, but that's what it looked like. One moment he was there, the next he was gone in a flash of light.

I was so tired, I was all thumbs, but I managed to get dressed. Jeans, T-shirt, mismatched socks (because I couldn't find matching ones), sneakers instead of my usual boots (because they didn't have laces), and basic weapons. No way was I entering fucking fairyland without my blades, though the ones I wore were special since regular weapons couldn't enter that realm. I also packed a lead-filled pistol. The Sidhe weren't fond of lead. At all.

My loins finally girded, I sent a quick text to Inigo to let him know where I was going. Then I shouted, "Yo, Kalen. Let's go."

A silver portal opened in front of me, and I stepped through.

# # #

The Sidhe lying on the narrow cot looked about a thousand years old. His skin was sallow and heavily lined, sagging off his skull like melted candle wax. Bloodshot eyes, the white yellowed with jaundice, stared back at me from sunken sockets. The stench of sickness and death hung heavy in the air. It was horrific. I expected to see such a thing in a human hospital, but not among the nearly immortal Sidhe.

Kalen grabbed my arm and pulled me from the room. Good thing too. I wasn't sure I could move from the shock.

The Otherworld was as breathtakingly beautiful as ever. Fully recovered from Morgana's evil reign, the sky was a soothing pale green that offset the richer jewel tones of the forests and streams. Her nephew was doing a much better job of the reigning thing. The castle of the Sidhe king had returned to alabaster shot with gold and silver, almost painful in its glory, the black sickness long forgotten. But the people...

Everywhere I turned, Sidhe were ill and dying. They lined the streets, begging for someone to save them. Apparently they thought that someone was me. I wondered if insanity was part of this illness. I was a killer, not a healer. I no longer winced at the thought, though maybe I should have.

"How, um, old is he?" I asked, turning for a last look at the dying Sidhe.

"He is one of my guards. Only five hundred years. He should be in his prime. Instead..." He shrugged and drew me down the hall.

I remembered Kalen's guards. They were chosen from the prime of the Sidhe. Big, muscular, handsome, and very, very deadly. Nothing like the wizened ancient I'd seen lying on that cot. "Why aren't you effected? Everyone else seems to be."

Kalen led me into a library and closed the door behind us. He sank into one of the chairs in front of the fireplace and stared into the amber flames for the longest time. I scanned the shelves of leather-bound books, but they were all written in Sidhe.

"I am affected," he admitted, "but the poison works its way much more slowly in me. The power of the king, I suppose. I still have time, but only a little." His tone and expression were grim. He looked tired. Mortal.

I shivered. "Poison?" I sank into the chair next to him. "I thought you said this was a sickness?"

"Metaphorical poison. As far as we can tell, there is no actual poison involved."

I frowned. "Has this ever happened before?"

"If it had, do you think I would have called on you?"

"Good point." I leaned my head back on the chair. It was so warm and cozy, I could have fallen asleep right there. I shook my head. There was no time. I had to help the Fae king. I owed him that. He'd helped me stop his aunt from destroying both our worlds. Granted, he'd had his own motives, but didn't we all? "When did this sickness start?"

"About a week ago. It was unnoticeable at first. A few of the lesser Sidhe began to feel weak, unwell. It was odd, but I assumed Morgana's influence still lingered. Then the stronger began to feel its effects, and it became increasingly worse. Nothing we did stopped the progression or spread of this disease."

"I still don't understand why you think I can help. I'm hunter, not a doctor."

"Ah, but it was your friend who started it."

I gave him a blank look. "My friend?"

"Kabita Jones."

I bolted upright. "You saw Kabita? When? Where?"

"Right here in this very room."

"But how did she get in? She'd need a portal."

"There was one open in Liverpool, thanks to a pair of idiots who thought a night on the town was a good idea." He shook his head in exasperation. "She jumped in and entered our realm. We spoke, and shortly after she left, the first of my people became ill. Unfortunately, she is now dead, so we cannot ask what she may have brought with her. Since you are investigating her death, I was hoping you could help with that."

I didn't bother asking him how he knew about Kabita's death or about my investigation. The Sidhe king had his ways. "Maybe that's why she was in Liverpool? For the portal?" Was that the thing she'd found wrong? Didn't seem like it, but anything was possible.

"Perhaps. I do not know. It may have been the reason, or simply a coincidence."

"What did she want to talk to you about?"

He frowned. "It was very odd. She claimed to be hunting a rogue dragon and seemed to think it was hiding in the Otherworld." He snorted. "As if we would allow such a thing."

"Maybe it used the portal, like she did."

"Impossible. Our portals do not allow other species to enter."

"Kabita seemed to travel it just fine."

He smiled a little. "There are certain humans we allow to pass through the portals." He gave me a pointed look.

"Okay, so she was here, she asked about this rogue, and then what?"

"I assured her he was not here. I even allowed her to question my men. It came to naught, and she left, albeit somewhat reluctantly. It was all rather odd."

"And you have no idea what happened to her after she left?"

"You mean, do I know who killed her or why? I'm afraid I do not." He gave me a look filled with sympathy. I didn't want his sympathy. I wanted answers, and it looked like solving his little crises might help me do that.

"All right, I'll do what I can, but I can't make any promises."

He nodded. "It's all I ask."

As I left the palace and stepped back through the portal, one thought plagued me: *What the hell was going on?*

Chapter 8

I expected to step out of the portal and into my living room. Instead I landed in a cave. It was a nice cave with smooth red walls, classic paintings in elaborate gilt frames, mahogany shelves crammed with books and scrolls, and thick Persian carpets on the floor, but a cave nonetheless.

I squinted in the dim light. "What the actual fuck?"

"Hello, little one." The voice was low and booming. I recognized it instantly.

Whirling around, I gave the speaker a glare. "Hello yourself, Marid. I repeat, what the fuck?" I was saying that a lot lately.

The Marid was a massive being. In his corporeal form, he looked like a nearly seven-foot tall, muscular man except he had red skin. And I mean *red*. Like the color of a tomato or a newly made brick. His long hair appeared black in the dim light, but I knew it was actually a dark green. His eyes were gold-green and eerily luminescent. He was, as his name implied, king of the Djinn.

Yep. You read that right. Genies. As in magic lamps and wishes, although that part of the mythos was disappointingly absent from my dealings with the Djinn.

"I need your help, Morgan."

"So you hijacked Kalen's portal? He's gonna be pissed." Portals could, technically, only be opened by the Sidhe ruler or a portal witch. The Djinn, however, were not originally of planet Earth, so it seemed the rules didn't apply.

"I apologize." He didn't sound sorry. "But my people... something is wrong." He stepped out from behind his massive, ornately carved desk and moved slowly toward me like an old man with arthritis.

Shit. This was sounding familiar. "Show me."

He nodded and led me out of the cavern and into one of the main tunnels that acted as a sort of thoroughfare for the underground city of the Djinn. This wasn't my first visit, so I expected to see the tunnels full of Djinn, scurrying to and fro, but the tunnel was eerily empty. I was getting a really bad feeling about this.

He turned to me. "I was sorry to hear about Kabita."

My spine stiffened. "How'd you hear about that?"

The Marid's expression didn't change. "I know many things."

"Don't worry," I said grimly. "Whoever did it is going to pay."

He gave me a long, searching look. "I am certain that is true."

As we approached our destination, I smelled the same stench of decay and death that had been in the Otherworld. Double shit. The Marid stopped in the doorway of another cavern. This one was several times larger than the one I'd landed in, but had the same smooth red walls. That's where the similarity stopped. Every inch of floor space was crammed with cots and sleeping pallets occupied by Djinn, moaning and crying. They looked awful, aged and wasted and terribly sick. Just like the Sidhe.

"Why are they in corporeal form? Why don't they shift?" The Djinn's natural state was one of pure energy. In that state just about any illness or injury would heal, not that the Djinn had a habit of getting sick, but they did sometimes go into battle. I'd seen their fierce fighting firsthand.

"They can't. They are stuck in this state." He looked grim. "And they are dying."

I glanced at him. He looked healthy enough. "Let me guess, it's effecting you, too, but more slowly."

He nodded. "As Marid, I am stronger than the rest, but I will not be able to hold it off for long. Not that it matters. Should this continue, I will have no one left to rule."

Shitdammit. "I was just in the Otherworld. The same thing is happening there."

His expression darkened. "I had a feeling."

"Really? Why?"

"Come." He led me back down the hall to his office, where he waved me into a chair. A fire crackled in an antique grate, but it gave off no heat. A cheerful illusion. He settled behind his massive desk, although with him behind it, it looked normal instead of the size of an airplane hangar. "I believe we are under attack."

"The Djinn?"

"Not just the Djinn, but the Sidhe, as well. Possibly other species. It's difficult to say."

"But why? By who?"

He shrugged. "That is, indeed, the question. This sickness that spreads among my people and now among the Sidhe is not natural."

"That's painfully clear. What do you think it is? A spell or something?"

He nodded. "That is my belief, though it would have to be a most powerful spell."

"Okay, let's start with who would be powerful enough to cast such a spell. A witch?"

He shook his head. "I have not seen anything like this since shortly after the fall of Atlantis. Even an entire coven of witches could not create a spell of this magnitude."

"Well, vamps can't cast spells. I doubt the Sidhe did it to themselves." A thought struck me. "Unless the illness there is blowback?"

"Doubtful. This does not have the mark of Sidhe magic either."

I'd have to take his word for it. "So who would be strong enough?"

"I do not know. A thousand years ago, there may have been someone, but not in this day and age. This is truly ancient and dark magic. It would take a magic worker the likes of which this world has not seen in many generations."

Just what I needed, a magic worker run amok, blasting supernatural species with ancient spells. As if I didn't have enough on my plate with my regular job and solving Kabita's murder, not to mention the peanut. Could life get any more complicated?

"You will help?" the Marid asked.

I nodded. What else could I do?

"Don't suppose you could send me back through the portal?" I asked.

"I'm afraid not. I can only manipulate the portal, not create one."

I sighed. Good thing I had friends in strange places.

# # #

Tommy Wahenaka was a medicine man who lived on the Warm Springs Reservation on the edge of Djinn lands in the high desert of Oregon. We'd been through a lot together, me and the old man. He'd trained me when I needed help to control my ever burgeoning powers. Powers I still missed.

The Darkness snapped, reminding me it was there. I soothed it. I swear sometimes it was like having a two-year-old living inside me.

Tommy also had a vast amount of knowledge of the supernatural. I was hoping I could pick his brains, then hitch a ride over the mountain. Not that I relished a trip in Tommy's bone-rattling old pickup, but beggars couldn't be choosers.

The walk from the caverns wasn't a long one, but by the time I approached Tommy's cabin I was exhausted, thirsty, and dripping with sweat. The door banged open before I reached the front porch.

"Morgan Bailey. I thought I felt you coming." Tommy grinned at me, dark eyes twinkling. The wind teased strands of the long, white hair that had escaped from the single braid down his back. He was dressed in blue denim from neck to ankle. Man loved his denim.

"Did you hear me cussing the whole way?"

He chuckled. "Come in. Have some tea."

What was with the man and tea? Every time I visited it was non-stop tea. Always herbal, too. Not a drop of caffeine.

I clomped up the steps to the front porch. Tommy gave me a quick hug and waved me inside. I stepped across the threshold and came to a dead stop. There was a man sitting at Tommy's kitchen table. I recognized him immediately. The Dragon King's assassin.

"Vane, what the hell are you doing here?

He stood as I entered, his expression stoic. He bowed slightly and with great gravity. Freaking fantastic. Was that what I could expect from now on? Annoying.

Tommy waved at Vane. "I take it the two of you know each other."

I nodded. "We met recently in Liverpool. You can imagine my surprise at seeing him in your cabin." I gave Tommy a pointed look. Maybe he would explain since Vane was being all silent and cryptic.

Tommy crossed his arms. "It's a long story."

"We were talking about you," Vane said.

"Oh, really?" I turned to Tommy, eyebrow raised.

Tommy raised his hands. "What can I say? I like to gossip."

I held back a bark of laughter. Tommy was the last person to spread gossip. The man took tight lips to a whole new level.

"Sit," he said, giving me a gentle push toward the table. "I'll get tea."

"Great." I plopped into a chair and stared at Vane. "How do you two know each other?"

"We don't," Vane admitted. "I was doing a background check."

I wrinkled my brow. "On who?"

"You."

That surprised me. "Why?"

Vane sat down slowly and gave me a long look. "The dragon kin need help and Drago claims you're the one to give it."

"So why the background check? Drago's known me awhile." Plus I was nearly family, but I didn't bother to point it out. Vane was already aware of that.

"The king is not himself of late."

I froze. "He's sick?"

Vane nodded. "As are many of our people."

My heart sank. "Why don't you have it, whatever it is?"

"I do, but I am very old and very powerful. I've been able to slow the progression for a time."

I stared, thinking this was no coincidence.

"Crap. It's spread." I leaned back wearily.

"What do you mean 'it's spread?' Are others affected by this sickness?"

Before I could answer, Tommy returned with a cup of hot swamp water for me and sat down with us. "Now, why are you here?"

Blunt and to the point, that was Tommy. "I've got this problem." I glanced at Vane, wondering how he was going to take this. How much did he know?

"Go ahead," Tommy said. "The boy knows things."

'The boy' looked to be a least thirty-five years old, but was probably several centuries older than that. Still, I wasn't about to argue with Tommy. I gave them a quick rundown of what I'd found in the

Otherworld and on Djinn lands, finishing up with, "Sounds like it's spread to the dragons, too, whatever this is."

Tommy glanced at Vane. "What you think?"

"I believe the tale of a rogue dragon was a smokescreen thrown up by whoever was responsible for Kabita's death and this illness." Vane looked even grimmer than before, if that were possible. "There is some serious dark magic at work."

I blinked. "How do you know? Are you a medicine man, too?" I didn't think dragons had such things, plus that seemed an odd thing for an assassin to be.

Vane stared at me. "Of course not. I'm a university professor when I'm not working for the king. I teach ancient mythology, but my specialty is the study of ancient dark magics. Of course, you don't announce that at prestigious universities if you want to keep your position for long."

"Oh." Color me surprised. I couldn't imagine him in a tweed jacket with leather elbow patches. I could see him lecturing a classroom full of kids, though. They'd either be swooning or wetting their pants. "So that's how you figured out this illness was magic based."

"Yes. I first began to suspect in Liverpool, but as I discussed the situation with Tommy"—he nodded at the older man—"then heard of your adventures, my suspicion turned to certainty."

"Do you know what kind of spell this is?"

"I need to do some research, but it does have a familiar ring to it."

"You finish your tea?" Tommy interrupted.

I glanced down at the cooling, brownish liquid. "Uh, yeah."

"Good." He stood. "I'll take you home. Vane will fly back to Scotland to do his research. We'll figure this thing out."

I hoped he was right because from the looks of things, we needed to figure it out sooner rather than later.

Chapter 9

We were nearly to my place when Tommy's cell rang. He handed it to me without looking. I glanced at the screen. Vane.

"This is Morgan." I winced as Tommy's truck hit a pothole and my butt hit a spring in the worn out seat.

"I have some information. At least I believe I am on the correct path." His voice sounded distant and tinny.

I grimaced. "How reassuring."

There was a pause. "Do you want to hear this or not?" Wow. The dragon could get snarky.

"Go ahead. I'm putting you on speaker."

Vane's rich baritone was crackly as it boomed over the tiny speaker. "I can't be 100 percent sure, but from my research, this matches an ancient Sumerian spell."

"Say what?" I stared at the phone as if I could see Vane through it.

"Sumerian."

"Yeah, I heard that," I snapped. "What makes you think it's Sumerian?"

Pages rustled in the background. "It's the results we're seeing. According to the texts I have, when

Sumeria was at its height, one of the major cities was having a supernatural problem."

"And that was?"

"Unclear. The text simply states that the city of Eridu was under siege from supernatural forces. After many days and nights of death and destruction, the En, or High Priest, of the god Anu devised a spell that would cause the supernatural beings— creatures normally immune to such things—to sicken and die. Within days of casting the spell, the supernatural army attacking the city was wiped out."

It did sound like what we were dealing with. "How the hell did someone get their hands on an ancient Sumerian spell? They're not exactly lying around in local libraries."

"That is the question, isn't it?" He sounded amused, which was the most emotion I'd gotten from him so far. "It could be a scholar or archeologist. Something of that nature. Someone studying the history of Sumer. Or it could be someone who has inherited it from an ancestor. The real question is, who in this day and age would have the power to wield such a spell? We're talking magic developed by the High Priest of Sumer. There are those who believe this priest was descended from the Atlantean priesthood. In any case, your ordinary magic worker could never cast such a spell."

"That's some serious magical mojo right there," Tommy agreed. "Pretty sure whoever did this is tapped into some epically dark shit."

No one I knew had that kind of power. Even if my friend, Emory, gathered her entire coven of portal witches, they couldn't pull of anything like that. Besides, who spoke ancient Sumerian these days?

"Thanks for the info, Vane," I said. "I think I know someone I can ask."

"Of course. Anytime. Keep me posted. I will continue research on this end." Vane hung up without bothering to say goodbye.

"I take it you don't want to go home," Tommy said, glancing at me out of the corner of his eye.

"Nope. I need to talk to Eddie."

Tommy nodded. A couple minutes later he swung his rattletrap old pickup into the parking lot of Majicks and Potions, Eddie Mulligan's New Age shop in the Hawthorne District of Portland. The tires spit gravel as he screeched to a stop. The building was an old house that had been painted sky blue. The paint was faded, but the third eye that took up half the front wall had recently gotten a new splash of color. It stared at me as if judging my worthiness.

"You want me to wait?" Tommy interrupted my thoughts.

"No, that's okay. I can have Inigo pick me up." Or heck, I could walk. I only lived a few blocks away.

And pregnant I might be, but I wasn't an invalid. "Thanks, Tommy."

"No problem. You need help, you let me know. Me and the kid got some tricks up our sleeves." The kid. Boy, I bet Vane would love that.

I grinned. "I'll remember that."

He drove off with a squeak and a squeal, and I climbed the front steps and entered the shop. The bell above the door jingled merrily as I entered.

The stench of incense hit me immediately, tickling my nose and eliciting a sneeze. My stomach roiled, then settled, and I breathed a sigh of relief that I wouldn't have to run for the bathroom.

Rows of shelves filled the large front room of Eddie's shop, every inch crammed with colored crystals, bottles of herbs, scented candles, and a hodge-podge of other goods necessary for the modern New Age practitioner. As usual the stereo system was cranking out a bizarre mixture of musical influences. A dulcimer attempted to harmonize with a harpsichord while kettle drums kept time. There was sort of a Native American/African tribal thing going on that was interesting, to say the least.

Through a narrow doorway, I caught a glimpse of the room where Eddie kept the books, tarot cards, and CDs. A middle-aged woman in a yellow caftan had her nose buried in a book of love spells. I wondered if she were desperate or a writer. Could go either way. She put the love spell book into her

shopping basket and grabbed an Encyclopedia of
Magical Herbs. I was going with writer.

Behind the long counter, where customers paid
for their purchases, Eddie Mulligan perched on a high
stool. He was wearing a pumpkin-orange waistcoat
with a gold watch fob and a pair of purple corduroy
pants. His ring of curly white hair stuck out in various
directions, and his round, cherubic face was wreathed
in smiles. I wasn't fooled by his innocent appearance.
I'd recently discovered Eddie was, in fact, one of the
immortal Titans. As in pre-gods Titans. Turned out
he was Poseidon's father-in-law. The knowledge still
blew me away. To me he was just my quirky little
friend who knew all kinds of interesting things.

"Morgan! What a surprise. How can I help you?"
Eddie beamed. "Want some tea? Cookies?" He
hopped off his stool and disappeared behind the
beaded curtain into the backroom before I could stop
him. I could hear him rattling around back there,
putting the kettle on.

I tapped my fingers on the counter impatiently
while I waited for him to return. He finally did, pot of
tea in one hand and a plate of homemade chocolate
chip cookies in the other. I never could resist
chocolate chip, so I snagged one immediately.

"We've got big problems." As I munched on the
cookie, I gave him a quick rundown of the illness
running through both the Sidhe and Djinn camps, not
to mention the dragons. Then I followed that with

what Vane had found out about the Sumerian spell. "Is there anyone alive today who has enough power to wield that kind of spell?"

He pondered a moment, eyes gone hazy and fingers tapping on the counter as he sipped his cup of tea. "I'm unaware of a single person with that amount of firepower. Other than myself, of course, and I have no bone to pick with either the Djinn or the Sidhe and certainly not the dragons. Balance, you know."

I did know. Eddie was all about balance in the world, and he was convinced the supernatural races were key to that balance.

"What about the princess?" I asked.

Princess Sharai was a ten-thousand-year-old, half-Atlantean and the last living member of the royal house of Atlantis. Long story, but basically she now lived among us normalish folk, *and* she held my powers of air, fire, water, and earth, which annoyed me no end, even though technically, I'd only been holding them for her.

"Sharai would likely have had the power," he admitted. "Back when Atlantis fell. But she's been out of commission for thousands of years. Her abilities are still regenerating after so long a sleep. I doubt she would have the strength at the moment, never mind her lack of motive."

He had a point there, but I made a mental note to question her anyway. No stone unturned and all that. Once upon a time, Alister Jones had seemed like a good guy with no motive to do evil. Look how that turned out.

"Okay, so what about a group of people?" I asked.

"More likely," Eddie agreed. "A conglomerate of magical practitioners fusing their powers for evil. But it would have to be a very large group. Vane is right. A witch coven, even a strong one, couldn't possibly wield that much power. Not alone." He frowned. "There could be demons involved in this one, pulling energy from the Hel Dimension."

There went the neighborhood. "Why would demons want to kill Sidhe or Djinn?"

"Why did Alister?"

Another good point. I hated to ask, but... "What about dragons? They don't like the Sidhe much. Could they have pulled this off and it backfired somehow?"

"Well, they might have motive. The races haven't always gotten along. Still don't. Technically they'd have the power, but this doesn't smell like a dragon thing, you know?" Eddie tapped the side of his nose. "They tend to be rather blunt about things. This is subtle. Too subtle for a dragon."

"What about a rogue?" I told him how Kabita had supposedly gone to Liverpool in search of a rogue. Granted, Vane and Jade had ruled that option out, but what if they were wrong? I had to ask.

"Even less likely. Rogues, while powerful, are generally 'losing their shit,' as people say nowadays. Their actions make little sense. And subtle? Not even a little. Besides, their powers are on the fade, believe it or not. Burning up even as they use them more. I don't think a rogue could pull this off, even if it managed to retain enough mental power to do so."

Jade and Vane had been right, then. This whole thing was getting more confusing by the moment. "Do you know of any active magical conglomerates? Any groups at all that might have a motive to destroy the supernatural races?"

He tugged at his goatee. "Off the top of my head? No, but I will ask around, see what I can find out."

"Thanks, Eddie. I appreciate it. But be careful, will you? Whoever is doing this is one nasty mother."

He grinned. "Don't worry about me."

I almost smacked myself in the forehead. Duh. Titan. The bad guys should be worried about Eddie, not the other way around.

"Before you go..." He ducked behind the counter and came back up with a plastic zipper bag filled with what looked like weeds. "This is for you."

I gingerly took the bag from him. "What is it?"

"Herbal tea. It will help with the unpleasantness."

It took me a moment to realize he meant my morning sickness. "Uh, thanks."

"Instructions are taped to the bag. Enjoy!"

86

Sure, and I was the Queen of the Fucking Fairies.

Chapter 10

"Morgan, where the hell have you been?" Inigo stood in the doorway looking fifty shades of furious.

"Hello to you, too." I pushed past him into the kitchen and dumped Eddie's bag of weeds on the counter. They should probably go in the trash, but honestly? I was willing to give anything a try these days. I snagged the kettle off the stove, filled it with water, and set it to boil. Time to face the music.

Inigo was glaring at me. His blue eyes swirled with gold. Oh, boy. His dragon was close to the surface.

"No biggie," I shrugged. "I had a hunt, and then I took a nap."

"And then?" He was literally tapping his foot.

I tried not to roll my eyes. Really I did, but something just took over.

"Morgan!"

"Inigo!" I might have mocked him a little, but he was getting on my last nerve.

Before he could open his mouth, the kettle shrieked. I pulled it off the stove, threw some of Eddie's weeds in a mug, and splashed in some hot water.

"I don't know why you're freaking out," I said as calmly as I could. The first sip of tea definitely tasted like mulch. I made a face and kept sipping.

"Maybe because you were gone for eight hours without telling anyone where you were and not answering texts or phone calls."

"Oh."

"Yeah. Oh." He crossed his arms. He was clearly blazing mad.

"I did send you a text," I said, remembering clearly that I'd done so before Kalen dragged me off.

Inigo smiled grimly. "True." He pulled out his phone. "Let's see what it says, shall we? 'Got to run. Back later.' Very helpful."

Oops. "Well, I'm sorry about that, but it wasn't entirely my fault."

"Do tell." Sarcasm practically dripped from his voice.

I frowned. "Stop being a dick, and I will."

He squeezed his eyes shut for a minute, then opened them with a sigh. "I'm sorry, but I was really scared, Morgan. After what happened with Kabita…"

I suddenly felt guilty. No wonder he was upset.

"I'm sorry," I said lamely, unsure what else to say. "Kalen sort of appeared and dragged me off to the Otherworld."

Thunderclouds rolled across Inigo's face, and his shoulder muscles flexed. "He what?" His tone was low and dangerous.

"He needed help. Him and the Sidhe. They're sick, Inigo. Dying."

That shocked him. "How?"

"We don't know how, but we suspect it's a spell, and it's somehow tied to Kabita's death."

"We?"

I told him the whole story, from Kalen dragging me to the Otherworld to my visits with the Marid and Vane, and the ride in Tommy's truck. I finished with the information I'd gleaned from Eddie.

"He thinks Sharai isn't involved, but I have to be sure."

"Wait until tomorrow. You need rest."

I wanted to argue, but he was right. I was drooping. "Fine. But I'm going first thing in the morning."

"Agreed. And I'm going with you."

"You don't have to do that. I'm perfectly fine on my own."

He gave me a long look. "We're a team, Morgan."

"Well, sure. Of course."

"Then it's time you treated me like it."

But I did. Didn't I?

"At least act like you trust me."

That was hitting below the belt. "I do trust you."

"Do you?"

###

The portal spit us out in the middle of a verdant field. A gentle breeze stirred grasses nearly as high as my waist. Dark trees edged the field, and in the distance I could make out the shore of a lake, its blue water shining in the late morning sun. I recognized the place from my one other visit to the state of Michigan. My last stand, if you will, against Alister and Morgana's evil.

I felt a pang. This was also where I'd lost my powers. All of them except the Darkness. Sometimes I still felt empty.

Inigo reached down and squeezed my hand as if he knew what I was thinking. Maybe he did.

"Well, well. I wasn't expecting visitors," The voice from behind sounded amused. We turned to see a tall woman with long hair that at first appeared auburn, but was dark plum when the light hit it.

"Hi, Sharai," I said casually, like I wasn't there to accuse her of murder. "How are things?"

Her eyes danced with humor. "Did you come all this way to ask how I'm doing? Or perhaps you came to check up on Jack?" She gave me a knowing look.

I barely refrained from sneering at her. Sometimes I didn't like Sharai very much. "I literally don't care. As long as the plans the two of you are hatching don't threaten to destroy the world, whatever." I gave her a long look. "Speaking of which—"

"Oh, dear." She sauntered toward us. "Don't tell me somebody else it at the apocalypse game. Hello, Inigo. You're looking delicious."

Inigo gave her a mild look. "Sharai." He actually had to hold my hand to my side. I wanted to rip her eyes out of her head.

I managed to get myself under control. Flies with honey, or whatever that saying was.

"Well, I don't know about an apocalypse," I admitted. "But someone is using an ancient Sumerian spell in an attempt to kill off the supernatural races. You wouldn't know anything about that, would you?"

She looked genuinely surprised and confused. "How would I know an ancient Sumerian curse? You do realize I was put into stasis nearly three thousand years before Sumer was settled, don't you?"

I was a little surprised she knew that much about history. She'd been in stasis for most of it. "Sure. But you could have gotten your hands on it somehow. Ancient texts or something."

"Okay, I'll play." She crossed her arms, her amusement growing. I knew she was toying with me, but I had a higher purpose. "Why would you consider me a suspect?"

Had she been watching crime TV? "Uh, because you're probably about the only person on earth right now powerful enough to cast the spell." Besides Eddie, maybe, and I knew he didn't do it. He didn't need ridiculous things like spells. He was power personified. One word, and he could wipe us all out. Probably.

Sharai frowned. "Why would I do this thing? It's so...unnecessary."

"Really? I don't know what your plans are. For all I know, you're jonesing to wipe out all supernatural species on this planet. Or maybe all species, for that matter."

"Oh, please." She marched across the field, her hips swaying in an annoying manner. I followed her closely, and Inigo followed me. "I have no interest in destroying anyone. My plans are for peace among all the races, and they're not immediate. This will all take a great deal of time." She eyed me. "You likely won't live to see it." She cocked her head to the side "Then again, maybe you will."

"What does that mean?"

She smiled mysteriously, which was irritating. "The answer to your question is no, I did not cast this spell. I don't know anything about it."

"Do you know who might have?"

She shrugged. "Of course not. I keep myself secreted away from the world, at least for now. I think you are—what is the expression? Barking up the wrong bush."

"Tree."

"What?"

"The expression is 'barking up the wrong tree.'"

She wrinkled her forehead. "Really? Huh. I wonder why?"

"You know. Bark. Trees."

"But dogs bark."

I sighed. "Never mind. Jack can deal with your English lessons. Where is he, by the way?"

She smirked in that grating way of hers. "Jealous?" Her eyes slid to Inigo, who remained stoic. That was one of the best things about him. Jealousy simply wasn't in his nature.

"Not even a little. Just curious." It was the truth, too. Maybe once upon a time, I would have been jealous, but Jack had burned those bridges, and I'd moved on to someone who actually gave a damn about me. It was a liberating experience.

"He is obtaining supplies at the moment. Would you like me to give him a message?"

"Don't worry about it. But you could do me a favor."

"What's that?"

"Open a portal back to Portland. I think my hay fever is about to go haywire."

# # #

After returning from Michigan and the interview with Sharai, Inigo insisted I stay home and rest. "You're looking peaky," he said, tucking me into bed with determination.

"Excuse me? What exactly is that supposed to mean?"

He sighed heavily. "Don't get all huffy."

I glared at him. Seriously? He was telling me not to get huffy?

"All I'm saying is it's been a long day. Hell, a long week. A little nap won't hurt anything."

"Except the last time I took a little nap, I got my ass dragged into the Otherworld." I didn't mention the visit from Kabita's ghost. That was nothing anyway. Just a dream. It was normal to have bad dreams after stuff like that happened to a friend, right? "Haakon needs me to do an upgrade on the computer system at the office, so I'll be gone awhile."

"You mean he wants you to hack into somebody else's computer system."

He grinned. "Something like that, but it's highly classified so—"

"I don't want to know."

"Promise you'll rest while I'm gone."

I looked him straight in the eye and said, "I will stay right here in this bed for at least, what, an hour?"

"Two."

"Fine. Two hours."

He nodded. "Good. I'll be back." He kissed me on the cheek and slipped out the door.

The minute I heard his car leave the driveway, I was out of bed. I padded into the kitchen, snagged my laptop off the table, and returned to bed. I was keeping my word. I'd stay right in bed like I promised. But I was using this time for some research.

I opened the laptop and began the hunt. Totally different type of hunt from hunting vamps, but I was semi-good at it.

Neither Jack nor Sharai had any sort of social media presence. Not surprising since Jack was a nearly immortal Sunwalker and former Templar Knight. That would have been all sorts of awkward. Sharai had no identification of any sort. Well, she had something Eddie whipped up, but there was no real depth to her cover as of yet. She didn't seem concerned, but advertising her presence wasn't in her best interests.

I searched various conspiracy websites for anything hinky going on in their neck of the woods. Other than a couple of UFO sightings and claims the government was spying using cow-cams, it looked like the two of them had been keeping a low profile. Still, it didn't mean they were innocent.

Another search for Atlantis and Sumeria revealed a lot of speculation that Sumerians were the remnants of the Atlanteans, which would seem to loop Sharai into the mix. However, Sharai had been put in stasis, for lack of a better term, long before the Sumerians came around, which technically sort of cleared her unless the Sumerian spell was much, much older than we realized. Could it actually be from Atlantis? Then Sharai might have had access to it or at least knowledge of it. And while Eddie might think she wasn't strong enough yet, she could have gotten others to help her. Sharai might claim she had no motive, but I was used to people lying to me. I couldn't scratch her off the list of suspects yet.

My phone rang, and I glanced at the screen. Eddie. "What have you got for me?" I answered without preamble.

"And a good afternoon to you, too." He sounded amused rather than offended. "I've reached out to my contacts, and as far as I can tell, there are no local magical groups that would have the power to pull off the sort of spell we're talking about."

"Damn. There goes another lead."

"I'm sorry," he said kindly. "I wish I could have been more help, but at least we've eliminated one avenue of inquiry."

"I guess so. By the way, are you absolutely sure Sharai couldn't have done this?"

"I'm sure, Morgan. I would have felt it, believe me. In some ways, the Titans and the Atlanteans are connected."

I wanted to ask him more about that, but before I could, he gave me a cheery goodbye and hung up. One of these days I was going to get Eddie to stop being mysterious and tell me things.

Suddenly a cracking yawn overtook me. I was far more tired than I'd realized. I was about to set my laptop aside and settle down for that nap Inigo wanted me to take when a small framed watercolor, hanging above my dresser, took a swan dive off the wall.

I don't mean it fell like a normal object: straight down. It lifted off the wall, flew through the air, and smashed to pieces at the foot of my bed. I stared at the broken glass, baffled. Surely I hadn't seen what I thought I'd seen.

My jewelry box upended next, spilling its contents across the dresser like a giant hand had batted it out of the way. A bottle of Inigo's cologne whizzed by my ear and shattered against the headboard. A cloud of spice and sandalwood engulfed the room to the point where I was choking.

When the bedside lamp levitated, that was it. I jumped out of bed and ran from the room like the hounds of hell were on my tail.

# # #

The door flew open before I could knock. A woman stood in the doorway, dark hair fixed in a bun with chopsticks, wearing a black silk robe covered in multi-colored dragons.

"Morgan!" She hugged me in a flurry of silk and perfume. "They told me you were coming."

I didn't bother asking who "they" were. Cordelia Nightwing had friends in high places.

"Good to see you, Cordy." I glanced over my shoulder to make sure I hadn't been followed by whatever had chased me around the bedroom.

"Come in, come in. How's the peanut?"

"Making me puke every five minutes, but otherwise fine," I said.

"Oh, don't worry about that," she said as she led me past overcrowded bookshelves and into her living room. "I've got a nice herbal tea that'll fix you right up."

I made a face. "Yeah, I got one of those teas from Eddie. Looks like weeds."

She laughed merrily, her voice carrying through the apartment. "Now you sit down, and I'll get some of that tea and a few cookies. Be right back."

I sighed. Guess I was drinking weeds whether I liked it or not.

Cordy's cat, Bastet, was in her usual spot in the middle of the couch. She glared at me as I sat in the chair across from her. Bastet was interesting. There was no other word for it. I swear that cat was sentient. Not in a normal cat way, but in an otherworldly, psychic, cat-goddess way. Although she and I had more or less come to terms, she still kind of freaked me out.

After giving me a good long stare, the cat closed her eyes and went to sleep. Apparently I was beneath her today. Nothing new there.

Cordy sailed back in, tea tray in hand. I smelled the weeds brewing, and my stomach gave a dangerous turn. Even the cookies didn't look terribly appealing.

Setting the tea tray down, Cordy gave Bastet an unceremonious shove before plopping down in the mound of decorative pillows on the couch. She poured tea into a cup and handed it to me, along with a plate of cookies. She was more confident about my eating abilities than I was.

"So you've got a mystery on your hands," she said without preamble.

"What have you heard?"

Her expression turned sad, her sapphire eyes a little watery. "I heard about Kabita. Oh, *they* didn't tell me. It's all the news down at Fringe."

Fringe was a nightclub frequented by the supernatural set. Cordy read tarot there most nights. There wasn't a thing in the supernatural world that wouldn't eventually end up as gossip at Fringe.

"I'm so sorry, Morgan."

A lump lodged itself in my throat, and I swallowed hard, ordering the tears to get back up those damn ducts. "I'm going to find out who did it." I said it with more confidence than I felt. The number of leads I had could be held in a thimble. My investigation was going absolutely nowhere.

"I'm certain you will, but that isn't why you came, is it?"

I didn't know why I was even surprised by comments like that anymore. "I think I'm being haunted or something."

She picked up a tarot card from the coffee table and fiddled with it, turning it over and over as if it would give her inspiration. "I was reading the cards this morning."

"And?"

She was quiet for a long moment. "You aren't wrong about being haunted. But don't worry, the ghost is gone. For now."

"The ghost?" Oh, joy. I had a bad feeling I knew who the ghost was, too. "It's Kabita, isn't it?"

"Yes."

"Well, I wish she'd just say 'hello' instead of throwing stuff around my bedroom. She nearly brained me with a cologne bottle."

"That is…unfortunate." Cordy seemed hesitant. "I'm sorry the news isn't better."

I gave her a long look. "What aren't you telling me?"

She closed her eyes a moment, as if in pain. When she opened them, the blue swam with unshed tears. "For now she just wants your attention, but soon she'll be coming to seek revenge."

"Well, good. I'll help her."

"No, Morgan, she's coming to seek revenge on you."

I stared at her for a long while. "That's insane. Why would she have reason to do that? She was my friend. My best friend. If she'd have come to me about whatever it was she was investigating, I would have helped her."

"I don't know. It's just what the cards say." She got up and walked over to one of the bookshelves and rummaged in one of her many trinket boxes.

I snorted. "You'll forgive me if I don't take their word for it."

She gave me a stern look as she returned, something clutched in her hand. "The cards never lie."

And that was the problem. They never did. "What do I do?"

She handed me a black cord. On it hung a small metal disk stamped with symbols: a pyramid, the sun, a cross. "This talisman will protect you from evil. Wear it always."

I lifted the cord over my head and let it fall into place, then tucked the disk beneath my shirt.

"Promise me, Morgan."

"I promise."

I had little faith in talismans, but I had a feeling I was going to need all the help I could get.

Chapter 11

There was one other magic worker in the city who might know if there was someone powerful enough to wield the spell. She might even know more about the spell itself. It was a long shot, but I was willing to try anything. I needed to figure this out and deal with Kabita before anything worse happened.

Emory Chastain came from a very long line of portal witches. The magic in her was strong, as it was in all her coven. Not enough for the spell, according to Eddie, but they had to be tapped into things. I knew they were friends with members from other covens, and sometimes they blended their powers.

I was halfway there when my phone rang. "Are you all right?" Inigo sounded calm, but I knew him well enough to know he wasn't.

"Of course, why?"

"I stopped by the house to check on you. The room looked like a tornado hit it and you were gone. You were supposed to be resting."

"I was, but then weird shit started happening."

"What kind of weird shit?"

I told him about the stuff levitating and flying around, and how I'd gone to Cordelia. I left out the part about Kabita coming for vengeance. He didn't need that on his plate.

"Where are you now?"

"On my way to Emory's. I thought she might be able to point me in the right direction."

"Why didn't you call me?"

"And tell you what? A ghost is smashing stuff in our house? I'm visiting a friend. Come on. You're not my babysitter."

He was quiet so long, it made me nervous. "No, Morgan, I'm not. But I do love you. Can you imagine how I felt when I saw the state of the bedroom? How I felt when I couldn't find you? How I felt when you didn't answer my texts?"

He'd texted me? Oh, crap. I'd been so busy doing my thing, I hadn't even noticed.

"We're supposed to be a team," he continued, "yet you keep treating me like an inconvenience."

"That's not true," I snapped. "I just… I'm used to doing things on my own. I forget." I winced even as the words came out of my mouth. "I didn't mean it that way. I just—"

"Tell Emory hello for me." Then he hung up.

Dammitall. I was going to have some making up to do. I sighed. Such was my lot in life lately. I really sucked at the whole relationship thing. Funny, because before I became a hunter, there was nothing I'd wanted more than the traditional white picket fence scenario. Now the whole relationship/baby/commitment thing was freaking me out.

I focused on the task at hand. I could deal with the drama in my life later. Much later.

I found Emory at her shop on Sellwood. The floor was made of wide wooden boards the color of coffee, the walls painted white and lined with glass shelves containing neatly organized vials of herbal tinctures and bottles of powder mixes. In the center of the room, beneath a crystal chandelier, a farmhouse table painted shabby chic white was piled with tins of herbal tea, candles, and homemade soaps. In one corner was a small alcove containing a low coffee table and two comfortable, purple chairs where Emory sometimes had consultations or read tea leaves for clients.

She came around from behind the counter, a concerned expression on her face. Her long, strawberry blonde hair hung like a veil around her shoulders, making her look almost ethereal. "Morgan, is there something wrong?"

What did it say about our relationship that the first thought in her head was that something was wrong? Of course, I only ever sought her out when something bad happened or we needed to use the portalways, but it seemed there should be more to our relationship than that.

"Nothing's wrong." I glanced around to ensure we were alone. We were. Must be the wrong time of day for herb and spice shopping. "I mean, there is, but not like you think." I quickly gave her an overview of the issue with the Djinn, Sidhe, and dragons, and how I believed it to be caused by an ancient Sumerian spell. "Do you know anyone at all who might be capable of wielding a spell like that, either on their own or with some kind of assistance?"

"Goddess." She looked a little pale, but it was hard to tell. She was always pale. She clutched a string of chunky turquoise beads hanging around her neck. "You're sure about this?"

"Saw the results with my own eyes."

"Okay, let me think about this." She paced back and forth, tapping her chin with her forefinger. The nails were painted turquoise to match her sandals and necklace. "I know of at least one coven that's into some strange stuff. I wouldn't say any of them were particularly powerful, but they've got a lot of members. I suppose if they could draw on the strength of all their members, plus tap into something supernatural like a demon or something, then...maybe." She sounded doubtful.

"It's a place to start. Give me the details."

She returned to the counter to scribble something on a sticky note. She handed me the bright yellow square. "Memorize this, then burn it. And do not let them know I was the one who sent you."

"Of course not. My lips are sealed."

"Anything else?"

"Uh, yeah. Don't suppose you could open a portal for me and Inigo tomorrow."

She lifted and eyebrow. "Again? I'm going to have to start charging you guys. Where to this time?"

"London. It's Kabita's memorial."

# # #

I stood back from the grave. I didn't want to look at it. I didn't want to think about Kabita being put into that deep, dark hole in the ground in Highgate Cemetery. I didn't want to think about her being dead, and I'd never see her again, never talk to her.

Her three brothers—Dex, Adam, and Adler— stood near the grave dressed in matching dark suits. They could have passed for triplets, but I knew Adam and Adler were the twins and Dex was older. The loss of their only sister clearly weighed heavily on them, and the lump that seemed to have permanently lodged itself in my throat doubled in size.

Next to the Jones boys was an older Indian woman with silver-streaked hair. She wore a white sari trimmed in rich bands of gold. I was betting she was Kabita's aunt, her mother's sister, and the only surviving female relative from that side of the family. It was from her mother's side Kabita had drawn her witchblood, and I knew it was strong in her aunt. I wanted to talk to her, but it felt awkward. They were family. I was an outsider.

I noticed that no one from Alister's side of the family showed up. Except for Inigo, that is. Not that he would ever lay claim to the relation. It ticked me off her father's side wouldn't acknowledge her. Were they embarrassed? Or pissed off about Alister? It didn't matter. They should be here. Family was family, after all, even when they tried your soul.

The Darkness in me rose, its cold anger fueling my own pain and rage. My vision narrowed to a pinprick as the Darkness encroached on either side.

Inigo squeezed my arm. *Easy, love.* His mind spoke to mine, a clever little trick of his dragon nature. I guessed he could sense my tension and anger. I willed myself and the Darkness to chill the fuck out. I didn't need to be going ballistic at a funeral. It wouldn't do anybody any good, and I'd likely end up with all of MI8 on my ass.

I knew immediately who they were. They tried to look normal, blend in with the other mourners, but it was clear they were agents. Three of them, two women and a man. He was blond, tall, and ridiculously Nordic. The women—one black and one Eurasian—were much shorter and deceptively dainty. I could practically smell the danger in them. I'd take on the male agent before I'd face either one of them.

"I need to talk to them," I whispered to Inigo. "They worked with Kabita. Maybe they know something."

He nodded slightly. "We'll make it happen."

The service dragged on until I was fidgeting, my feet sore from unaccustomed heels. The priest wouldn't shut up until it started to drizzle and one of Kabita's brothers finally put a kibosh on the long-winded speech. I wasn't the only one who sighed in relief.

As the mourners trickled away in small groups, Inigo and I waited for the three MI8 agents. We followed them as they left, sticking close behind. Several yards down the path, they stopped and whirled on us almost as one. Creepy.

"Who are you and why are you following us?" the black female agent snapped at us stridently. I would have been scared if not for the fact I was a hunter.

I gave her a long, dark look. "Morgan Bailey. Inigo Jones."

The woman's eyes widened, and she glanced at her compatriots. The other two bore twin expressions of astonishment. Oh, goodie. I loved freaking people out.

"Morgan?" the man asked, stepping forward. "The hunter?"

"I take it you've heard of me?"

More exchanged glances. "You could say that," he said.

"Kabita mentioned you," the Asian woman said. "Several times."

I lifted an eyebrow. Both went up, of course. Curses. One of these days I would master the one brow lift. "Did she? All bad I hope."

Her lip quirked with amusement. "She said you were difficult."

"Sounds like something she would say."

The three of them continued to eye me like a bug under a microscope. It was off-putting, to say the least.

"So…" I gave them a long look. "You got names?"

"I'm Agent Dorsey," the black woman said. "This is Agent Mills and Agent Chin." She nodded to the man and the Asian woman in turn.

"Nice to meet you," I chirped perkily. That's me. Perky as fuck. "The reason I was following you was that I wanted to talk to you guys about Kabita."

"Why? We don't know anything," Mills said defensively. His accent had gone from posh London to slightly northern. Interesting.

"You worked with Kabita. I'm assuming rather closely, or you wouldn't be here."

They nodded reluctantly.

I gave them a hard look. "Why was she in Liverpool?"

"To hunt a rogue, of course," Mills said.

"Don't lie to me. I know there was no rogue."

The three exchanged glances again. "Are you trying to solve her murder?" Chin asked softly.

"You betcha."

She turned to the others. "Tell her."

Dorsey sighed. "For the first few weeks everything was normal. Well, as normal as things could be what with trying to fix everything Alister Jones fucked up. One day I caught her going through some old files. She seemed startled, like she didn't want to be seen." Dorsey shrugged. "She stuffed the files away and acted like nothing had happened. It was suspicious."

"Did you ever find out what those files were?"

"Unfortunately, no," Dorsey admitted. "But over the next couple of weeks, Director Jones became increasingly obsessed with something. She spent hours at a time shut up in her office, speaking to no one, allowing no one in. When she wasn't in her office, she'd be gone. No one could reach her."

Director Jones. Had a weird ring to it. "Then what happened?"

Mills took up the tale. "She became increasingly anxious, snapping at people, carrying her firearm everywhere."

"I thought guns were illegal in the UK?"

"They are," he said. "Except for special police and agents like us."

"Okay. Go on," I urged.

"One evening I was working late. I went to get a coffee and saw her coming out of her office with a backpack in her hand. I asked where she was going, but she ignored me." He grimaced as if still stung by her dismissal. "She left the building so I followed her out of curiosity."

I'd have followed her too. "Where'd she go?"

"She got in a cab," he said. "That was the last any of us saw or heard from her."

Chin cleared her throat. "Not exactly true."

The other two stared at her. "What?" Dorsey sounded as stunned as she looked.

"I got an email from her two days after she left London," Chin explained. "She wanted me to look up something for her."

"What was it?" I asked.

Chin opened her mouth to answer, but before she could say anything, her head snapped back, blood sprayed all over her fellow agents, and she crumbled to the ground. A split second later, I heard the shot.

"Down!" Inigo shouted, grabbing me and practically slamming me into the gravel walkway. "Everybody down!"

The other two agents hit the ground. Neither of them seemed to be carrying a weapon.

"Where are your guns?" I yelled.

"We don't carry them unless it's necessary," Dorsey said.

"Well, don't you think *now* is fucking necessary?"

Mills was silent, eyes a little too wide. He'd gotten the bulk of the blood spatter. Looked like there were brains on his jacket, too. I was trying not to think about it. I was dangerously close to puking.

More shots rang out, bullets striking the ground inches from my face. "Off the path," Dorsey shouted. "Into the trees."

Staying low, the four of us scrambled off the gravel path and onto the grassy lawn. The tree line was mere feet away. Mills grunted and hit the ground.

"Damn." He was cussing so he was still alive, thank the gods. He staggered a bit but made it to the tree line as bullets kicked up chunks of turf around us.

Once behind a large grouping of oak trees, we stopped to catch our breath. Mills had his tie off, and Dorsey was wrapping it tightly around his upper thigh. It was bloody, but it looked like the shooter had missed any major arteries.

"What the fuck is going on?" I snarled.

"Apparently someone thinks we're getting too close to the truth," Inigo said.

"What truth? We know jack shit." I whirled on Dorsey. "What was Chin going to tell us? Do you know?"

"Sorry, no." Her expression was pinched, grief heavy in her eyes. "Maybe back at the office, we'll find something on Chin's computer."

"If we make it back to the office," Mills said grimly. White bracketed his mouth, and his pale gray tie was a dark burgundy.

"We're going to make it," Dorsey snapped.

"She's right, we are. But first we need to know who is shooting at us and why."

Inigo grabbed my arm as I started to rise. "No. Let me."

"Inigo—"

"You're pregnant, remember? And you're not bulletproof."

"Neither are you."

"Sure I am." He gave me a wicked grin.

"Oh."

His grin got bigger. "Exactly."

There was a shimmer, and a blue dragon the size of a large horse stood where Inigo had been a moment before. Mills looked like he was going to pass out. Dorsey didn't even bat an eyelash.

I'll find our attackers and teach them a lesson.

"Go get 'em," I said.

He launched into the air, and Mills' mouth hung open. "Er, your boyfriend is a dragon."

Way to state the obvious, Mills. "Yep."

"And he's going after the people who are shooting at us." Dorsey said.

"Yep."

"And he's bulletproof?" she asked.

"Essentially, yes."

Her eyes turned dark and a look of satisfaction spread across her face. "They better run."

Chapter 12

We took off for the parking lot, running hell-bent for leather, hoping to distract the shooters so they wouldn't spot Inigo. I was really missing my weapons. All I had was a small boot knife and my wrist sheaths, the only things I could wear to a funeral without looking more than a little out of place.

Another shot rang out. The bullet plowed into the ground narrowly missing my foot. "I thought guns were illegal."

Sweat glistened on Mills' forehead. "They're using hunting rifles," he said.

Which meant half the countryside owned the damn things. Our attackers could be anybody.

"This way," Dorsey panted. "I've got weapons in the boot."

That was English-speak for the trunk of her car.

We followed the tree line toward the parking lot, using the trees as a screen between us and the shooters. Occasionally a bullet would smack into a trunk and send bark flying.

"We still don't know who we're fighting," Mills said.

"Like it matters?" I snapped. "They're shooting at us."

He looked embarrassed. "Right."

The parking lot was in sight when Dorsey went flying face-first into a thicket of bushes. Mills was next. It was as if some giant had picked him up and hurtled him through the air. He landed several feet away. I was pretty sure he was still alive, but I couldn't swear to it.

I stumbled to a stop, glancing around. No one in sight.

"Okay," I said. "You've got my attention. Show yourself."

For a moment, nothing. Then a form shimmered in front of me.

"Kabita?" I whispered, stunned. It was her ghost. Kind of translucent, but her.

"You did this." Her voice was a crackling hiss, her eyes pools of infinite black. She didn't seem quite herself. It was more than a little freaky."Did what?" I had no idea what she was talking about.

"You killed me."

"No, I didn't. I don't know who did, but I promise I'm going to find out."

"Liar." She flew at me so fast I didn't have time to blink, much less get out of the way. I stumbled back, but her hands were around my throat, squeezing. I couldn't breathe. Little black spots danced in front of my eyes as I gasped and clawed at her hands. I was on the verge of losing consciousness, and if that happened, I was dead. How was she doing this? How could I stop her?

Cordy's gift! I reached under my blouse and pulled out the necklace. I managed to get it clear of the fabric but only just.

The light caught the talisman as it touched Kabita's hand, and the metal disk lit up like a supernova. There was a scream so loud, I swear it broke an eardrum. Then the light faded, Kabita's ghost was gone, and I slid to the ground.

# # #

I came to with Dorsey and Mills standing over me, twin expressions of concern on their faces.

"What the hell happened?" Mills blurted.

Dorsey was more practical, helping me into a sitting position and checking my vitals. Whatever she found must have satisfied her. "That was a ghost, wasn't it?"

"Yeah," I admitted. "Kabita's ghost."

They looked shocked. "But she tried to kill you," Mills said.

I sighed. "Maybe she's been affected by the spell."

Dorsey frowned. "Spell?"

I quickly explained the spell working against the Djinn and the Sidhe as she helped me to my feet. I was feeling woozy, if I were honest, so her help was appreciated.

"Bollocks," Mills said with feeling. "Is that what killed her?"

I shrugged. "I have no idea. Maybe."

"I don't understand," Dorsey said. "The spell kills supernatural creatures, it doesn't turn them homicidal."

"I know," I admitted. "But she's not herself and ghosts generally behave like the people they were in life. The spell is the only thing that makes sense to me." Maybe I was hanging onto a thread, but it was all I had. I couldn't believe that Kabita had turned evil of her own free will.

"Shooting's stopped," Mills said. Hopefully that meant Inigo had reached the shooters.

"Well, if Kabita is under some kind of spell, we need to free her of it," Dorsey said, helping me toward the parking lot. "We can't let one of our own get stuck for eternity like that."

I agreed with that wholeheartedly. "I'm working on it."

"What was that thing?" Mills asked. "It chased her away."

"A friend of mine gave me a talisman to protect against evil. I guess it worked." Although it made me sick to think of Kabita, or her ghost, as evil. How had this happened?

We had reached the cars before Inigo returned. He was only very slightly out of breath, picking random bits of grass and leaves from his suit.

"How'd it go?" I asked, propping myself against the car and pretending I was fine. No use worrying him.

He grimaced. "They got away."

I stared. "From you? In dragon form?"

"Even I can't control traffic. Not without exposing myself."

Well, crap. "Did you get a good look at them?"

"Not enough to know if they were human or something else."

Double shit. But it couldn't be a coincidence, Kabita's ghost attacking at the same time someone was shooting at us.

Inigo's eyes narrowed. "What's that on your neck?"

I automatically touched the sore spot where Kabita had been squeezing. I must have a glorious bruise by now. Before I could explain, Mills opened his mouth and blabbed the whole thing. Wimp.

Inigo gave me a long look. "You're okay?"

"Of course." More or less.

"The baby?"

"Fine." I'd have been able to sense if it wasn't. The peanut and I had a thing. I could sort of sense not thoughts, exactly, but emotions. Much like with Inigo only not as clearly. I was guessing it was the baby's quarter dragon blood. Right now, the kid was as pissed as I was. "We're fine," I assured him.

"Why would Kabita's ghost try to kill you?"

"I think she's been effected by the spell. She didn't look right."

He nodded as if it was a perfectly normal thing for a relative to be overcome by an evil spell and try and kill his girlfriend. I guess, in a way, it sort of was.

"Come on," Dorsey said. "Let's get back to the office. Maybe Chin was shot because she knew what was going on."

"I'll stay here," Mills said. "Handle clean up."

"You need a hospital," Dorsey argued.

"I'm fine. Somebody needs to handle this."

I cringed a little at the thought of him having to cover up the death of a colleague. The poor woman. It wasn't just supernaturals getting sick—as if that wasn't bad enough. But humans were being murdered, and I was still no closer to the truth.

Chapter 13

MI8 was still located in the same Georgian mansion I'd visited long ago with Kabita. Alister Jones had been in charge then, before he'd gone bad, or rather before we knew he was bad. The man had been rotten to the core. I hated thinking that Kabita had gone the same way. I assured myself it was just the spell, but it worried me. What if it wasn't?

Dorsey led us up the stairs and through a security door into a large bullpen. A dozen desks with glowing computer screens sat silent. Everyone was probably at the wake. Or the pub.

We followed her to a desk on the far side of the room. There was nothing personal on it, just neatly stacked files and orderly rows of office supplies. The bulletin board behind the desk was devoid of pictures or quotes or other things that people used to personalize their workspace. The only decorative item was a calendar. The current month had a picture of a sunset beach. I wondered if it had spoken to Chin on some level, or if she'd bought it because it was on sale. Based on the austerity of her desk, I was guessing the later. Sad.

Dorsey sat down in front of Chin's computer and tapped a few keys. "I'm in."

"You know her password?" I asked, though why I should be surprised I didn't know.

She shrugged. "Sure. And Mills'. Figured it would come in handy. What am I looking for?"

"You said she got an email from Kabita," Inigo said. "That would be a good place to start."

Dorsey's fingers flew over the keyboard. "Damn. Looks like she deleted it. And emptied the trash."

"Would it still be on the servers?" Inigo asked.

"Maybe. They're down in the basement. I can take you there."

"Don't bother. I'll find my way." And with that he slipped out of the room and down the hall.

She stared after him. "He does realize there are biometric scanners on all the doors, doesn't he?"

"Yeah. I wouldn't worry about that. Anything else interesting on Chin's computer?"

Tapping sounds filling the room. A faint line appeared between her brows as she concentrated.

"How long have you been with MI8?" I asked. It was partly idle curiosity, but I also wanted to know more about this woman. How well had she really known Kabita? Had she been here when Alister Jones nearly destroyed the world?

She didn't look up. "Not long. A little over two years. Dex recruited me."

That would have been while Alister was in charge. It was his son, Kabita's eldest brother, who brought Dorsey on board. That was a relief. Dex was a good guy. Of course, I'd thought that about Alister once upon a time.

"Well, this is interesting," Dorsey said.

"What?" I leaned over to get a look.

"She deleted her browser history but those things are easily recoverable." Dorsey tapped the screen with a fingernail. "See there? Looks like she was researching ancient Sumerian culture. History buff, maybe?"

I doubted it. Based on what I now knew, Chin had known something of what was going on. "Anything else?"

Dorsey shrugged. "Some stuff on dragons. No surprise there, though what she expected to find beyond what we've got in our system is beyond me. Our records are quite thorough."

Thanks to Alister, no doubt. He'd have liked nothing better than to wipe out the dragons, along with the other supernatural races.

"She was also digging into the backgrounds of some interesting groups."

"Like?"

"This global wiccan group keeps popping up in her searches. Temple of Gaia. Looks like they're pretty active in the green movement, but otherwise they don't stand out much. Can't imagine what she'd be looking into them for."

I could. A global organization of magic practitioners might have enough juice to pull off a spell like the one Vane had told me about, but I couldn't imagine a group devoted to the environment, nature, and healing magic being behind such a thing. I filed it away just in case.

"Any other groups of interest?"

"Daughters of Ishtar. Can't imagine they're anything to worry about. They're a small group. Half a dozen members from the looks of it."

My ears perked up at the Sumerian connection. Even I knew that Ishtar was the ancient Sumerian goddess of fertility and a bunch of other stuff. But why on earth would fertility goddess worshippers get involved with such dark, horrible magic?

"There's also the Esoteric Divine Worshippers of Ra." Dorsey snickered. "They mostly look like a bunch of wishful thinkers. Doubt they've got a magic bone between them."

She might be right, but it was still worth checking them out. They were local, too. "Can you print off their details? I'd like to set up a meeting with them."

She snorted. "Probably a waste of time, but sure." A few more key taps, and the printer was spitting out pages of information. Probably more than I needed.

"Let's have a look in her files, too."

"You got it." Dorsey clicked on the file icon and brought up a list of files. She opened them one at a time. "Pretty ordinary stuff here. Basic forms. Operation reports. Expenditure records."

"Anything on Kabita or Sumeria?"

"Not that I can see."

Dorsey was shutting off the computer when Inigo returned.

"Anything?" I asked.

"I was able to recover the email and print it." He handed me a single sheet of paper.

It was an email from Kabita to Agent Chin dated the day before Kabita's death in Liverpool. There was no greeting. Just one line:

I think I know what's going on.

# # #

Outside the car window, trees whizzed by in a blur of green. The sky was grim and gray, but the rain had yet to fall. I'd no doubt it would soon enough. I was feeling tired, queasy, and cranky, but I kept my mouth shut. No use dumping my crap on Inigo.

For whatever idiotic reason, the Esoteric Divine Worshippers of Ra insisted on meeting in the middle of nowhere outside a Podunk British village with the charming name of Steeple Piddington.

As Inigo pulled into the narrow lane that ran through the center of the village, I found myself surrounded by quintessential English charm. The street was lined with cottages, many of them thatched. Their stone walls and small windows with boxes overflowing with flowers were warm and inviting.

Halfway up the lane, the houses gave way to a small assortment of businesses. Most prominent, of course, was the pub—the White Horse. A hanging sign with an image of a white horse in front of a sunburst swung gently in the breeze.

"What do you want to bet one of the Esoteric people own that pub?"

Inigo glanced at me. "Why do you say that?"

I pointed. "The sunburst. Ra is the sun god, after all."

"Makes sense. Might be a good place to gather information."

More like he wanted a pint of something cold and yeasty. Me, I just wanted out of the damn car.

Across the street from the pub was a small market. Out front was a display of fresh fruits and vegetables. Through the open door I made out displays of sweets and snacks. Next to it was a charming little tea shop that was, unfortunately, closed.

Inigo pulled the car into the pub parking lot, and I breathed a sigh of relief. I nearly bolted from the car, my stomach lurching with every step.

"You all right, love?" he asked, sympathy in his eyes.

"I'll be fine. Just...the motion." I must have been a little pale, because he wrapped one arm around me and helped me toward the pub.

"Let's get you inside. I'll bet they have ginger ale. Maybe some salty potato chips."

I stared at him.

"What? I heard they help."

I'd never heard of such a thing, but I was willing to try just about anything.

The pub was dim and warm with a low-beamed ceiling dark with age and centuries of smoke from the inglenook fire. The bar was worn smooth from generations of elbows. Unfortunately, the stench of stale beer and cooking meat turned my stomach. I darted from the pub so fast, I left Inigo gaping after me.

I plopped down at a picnic table and sucked in deep breaths of cool, country air, glad it hadn't started raining. Gods, this kid was going to be the death of me.

A few minutes later, Inigo joined me with a can of ginger ale and a bag of chips in one hand, and a pint of beer in the other. He set down his offerings and gave me a good once-over. "How are you feeling?"

"Better. Sorry, the smell—"

He smiled. "I get it." He glanced up. "This is Miles. He owns the pub."

The man standing next to the table was as round as he was tall and had approximately twelve strands of hair dyed black and combed carefully over his bald pate. I wondered if he thought he was fooling anyone.

"Miles is also the High Priest of the Esoteric Divine Worshippers of Ra." Inigo's lip twitched. He was as amused by this as me.

"Mr. Miles," I greeted him solemnly.

"Oh, just Miles," he said with a grin, plopping down on the seat across from us. "Now, what can I do for you fine folks?"

"Well," I said, taking a careful sip of my ginger ale, "we heard about your organization and were curious."

His eyes narrowed. "Are you a reporter?"

"Heavens no. Merely someone curious about the ways of the supernatural. I was told you were the man to speak to."

He beamed with pride. "That I'd be."

"What exactly do you of the Esoteric Divine Worshippers of Ra do? Spiritually, I mean."

He leaned back, cleared his throat, and launched into a wildly detailed explanation of ancient Egyptian sun worship. "You see, the sun is the bestowed of light and life. The Great Cosmic Lightbulb in the sky. And Ra is his avatar on Earth. Praise be!" He lifted his hands toward the gray sky and gestured wildly. "It's essential to make offerings to Ra every day, just as the Egyptians did."

I'm not sure the ancient Egyptians would have recognized any of the practices Miles was describing, but no use offending the man, even if he was a little cuckoo.

"What kind of offerings?" I asked, wondering if human sacrifice was on the menu.

"I find Victoria sponge cake works well."

Was he serious? "Victoria sponge?" Trust me, it was delicious. Buttery vanilla sponge cake layered with whipped cream and jam. It was a British favorite, but I couldn't imagine that the ancient Egyptians knew anything about it or had offered it to their god.

"But of course." Miles beamed at me. "Ra has a sweet tooth."

"If you say so," Inigo mumbled under his breath. Miles either didn't hear him or pretended not to. Instead he prattled on about holy days and carving idols from soap, and I don't know what else.

"Do you do spells and things like that?" I asked when I could get a word in edgewise.

His eyes widened. "That's what I've been explaining to you."

"No, sorry. I mean, do you cast spells on, say, other people? Like curses or love spells or whatever."

That surprised him. His brow furrowed. "Goodness no. Why would we do that?"

"Lots of faith practices do. Some call them prayers, others magic. Amounts to the same thing, quantumly speaking." I wasn't sure 'quantumly' was a word, but I was going with it.

"That would be messing about with free will," Miles explained in a patient tone. "We don't believe in that sort of thing."

"So you wouldn't mess around with an ancient Sumerian spell, for instance?"

"Crikey, no. Don't want to be fooling with that nonsense. Dangerous, if you ask me."

He seemed genuinely appalled at the idea, and from what I could tell, he had no magical abilities. He was just an ordinary person practicing a rather unorthodox form of religion. Question was, were his followers the same?

"Is there any way I can meet with your group? Experience one of your rituals?"

He mulled it over, pulling at his lower lip. "I'm sure it would be fine, but our next ritual isn't for several weeks."

"Maybe I could come back?"

"But of course. I'll email you the details."

"Well, thanks for your time," I said. "It's been very enlightening."

He beamed. "Any time." He stood, preparing to go back inside. "Feel better. Perhaps a little sun worship would do you good." With a wink he was gone, back inside his pub.

"Guess we're back to square one," Inigo mused.

"Not quite. We've still got two other groups to check out, plus the Portland coven Emory told me about."

He nodded. "Let's return the car and take the portal home. You need to rest."

"Right. Because puking my guts out every five seconds is so restful."

Chapter 14

I tried to take a nap when we got home. Really I did. But sleep eluded me. My mind rolled over and over, reviewing everything I'd learned. It wasn't much, unfortunately. I still had avenues to investigate, but I wasn't feeling hopeful.

I finally gave up and climbed out of bed. Inigo had left for the office—Haakon had needed some computer expertise—so what he didn't know wouldn't get my ass thrown back in bed.

I sat at the kitchen table with a cup of decaf coffee and flipped open my laptop. First, I emailed Vane about the Esoteric Divine Worshippers of Ra. I guess I figured they were British and he lived in Scotland, so maybe he knew something. Then I opened up my browser and started searching.

It took no time at all to look up The Temple of Gaia's website. There was a lot of ranting about the sacredness of the Earth. Not that I disagreed, but ranting rarely got anyone anywhere. It looked like a combination of nature worshippers and green activists. Fairly extreme ones, too. Would they be willing to use a dangerous spell to protect Gaia? Probably. Question was, did they have the ability to do so?

The group was global and mostly online, but they had meetings in a few of the bigger cities. Portland didn't have an official one, although there were a couple of local members. I looked up their email addresses in the directory and sent them messages, asking to meet. I didn't mention ancient Sumerian spells or dying races. I pretended to be interested in spiritual things and said the Temple had caught my interest. I wanted to check it out and talk to some members before I joined.

Almost immediately, someone emailed back. She seemed eager, and we arranged to get together at a tea shop in Multnomah Village the following day.

One thing checked off my list. Emory had given me the email address of Hannah, the leader of a local coven, so I sent her a message, too.

My email alert pinged. It was a message from Vane confirming that he was aware of the Esoteric group and that they had zero magic. Great. There went that group of suspects.

I was on my second cup of decaf when Hannah messaged me back, inviting me to a coven gathering that night. I was going witching.

# # #

The coven met, interestingly enough, at a local church. The large stone building stood solemnly in the midst of a neighborhood of older houses, mostly

Craftsman and Victorians. It felt like it belonged somewhere in Europe rather than in the middle of urban America.

The walls were made of neatly cut stone. The dark wood ceiling soared high above, braced with massive wood beams stained to match. At the front of the church was a stained glass window depicting the dove of peace with an olive branch in its mouth surrounded by explosions of colored glass lit up by the late afternoon sun.

I was more than a little surprised that a church would allow a coven of witches to meet on their property. Churches were generally against that sort of thing. Maybe this one was just super progressive. I mentioned it to Hannah, the coven leader.

She laughed wickedly. "Oh, honey, they have no idea what we are. The Sisterhood of Portland Craftswomen. How innocuous does that sound?" She grinned.

"That doesn't sound very witchy."

She laughed again. Hannah was about sixty and dressed neatly in perfectly pressed light gray slacks and a silky white blouse. Her dainty pearl earrings and matching necklace were lustrous against bronze skin and silver hair. I'd imagined someone more like Emory. Bohemian. Hannah was elegant and professional, like she was about to host a town meeting or deliver the news.

"Not what you expected, huh?" she asked, amused.

What? Was she a mind reader?

"No mind reader. You have a very expressive face."

Dammit all. "Sorry. I've known a few witches in my time. You're not quite what I pictured."

"You must remember practitioners come in all shapes and sizes, and from all backgrounds. You never know who among us is harboring a secret light." She gave me a long look. "Take you, for instance. One would never guess you harbor Darkness in your soul."

I swear my jaw hit the floor. "How did you know?"

"I can see it. Fortunately for you, I also realize what it is, or you would have never entered this church."

Well, that was a cheerful thought. It was my turn to give her a long look.

"You're wondering if I'm strong enough to stop you," she said. Her face was expressionless. "Not on my own. But together, we are strong."

Interesting. They fit, at least ability-wise. I decided to dive in. Hannah seemed to appreciate bluntness. "Would you be strong enough to cast an ancient Sumerian spell?"

She cocked her head. "What sort of spell?"

"Something very, very powerful. And very, very old."

"How powerful?"

"Enough to sicken and kill three very nearly immortal races."

Her eyes widened. "The dragons?"

It was my turn for surprise. "You know about them?"

"And others. Is it them?"

"They're one of them. Though they're not as badly effected as others."

She seemed relieved. "I have friends among the dragons. Who are the others?"

That shocked me. It was rare that humans mingled with dragons enough to be friendly. "The Sidhe and the Djinn."

"Oh sweet goddess." She sank down on a nearby metal chair. "The Sidhe are bad enough, but the Djinn?" She squeezed her eyes shut as if in pain. "How is that even possible? They're not of this earth." She opened her eyes and stared at me as if I might have answers.

I was surprised she was so knowledgeable. Sometime I was going to pick her brain, but now was not the time. "I don't know. Experts I've spoken to agree a spell is causing this, and their best guess is it's one from ancient Sumer."

"Which means you would need an incredibly powerful magic worker to wield it. I can see now why you would want to question me. You're wondering if my coven is powerful to cast such a thing."

"Yes."

She sighed. "It's possible. Working together, all of us *might* be able to pull it off, but we have no reason to do so. I can't see how it would benefit us in any way. In fact, it would endanger the coven."

"How?" I asked with a frown.

"You don't know?"

"Know what?"

"All magic in this universe is interwoven. It's interdependent, like one enormous organism. If one part of the organism becomes ill and dies, the rest of the organism is in grave danger."

My eyes widened. "You're telling me if the Djinn or the Sidhe die, you will too?"

She nodded. "Eventually the disease will spread among us all, killing us one by one." Her expression was grim. "And believe me, you're not immune."

That startled me. "What do you mean?"

"Morgan Bailey, you *are* magic, and what kills magic will also kill you."

Chapter 15

The following day I sat at a small, round table in Medley, the only tea house in Multnomah Village, back to the wall, eyes glued to the window. I could easily see the entry and anyone who approached the building from where I sat.

At 2pm on the dot, a twenty-something with ragged, long, brown hair and wearing baggy cargo pants walked in. She headed straight for me, a pleasant smile on her round face. Her eyes behind her black rimmed glasses were hazel and framed by pale lashes. She blinked at me owlishly.

"Morgan?"

"Yes. Emily?"

She plopped down in the chair across from me and grinned. Her two front teeth were a little crooked which was oddly charming. "You bet."

She rummaged around in her worn backpack and pulled out a brochure. It was obviously printed on a home printer that had been in the process running out of ink. She handed it to me. "Some info on the Temple."

"Thanks."

As I flipped open the brochure, our waitress appeared looking a little frazzled and took our order for tea and scones before disappearing into the kitchen. I hoped she'd return soon. I was starving.

"Interesting," I said as I perused the brochure. "It looks like Greenpeace only with a Wiccan twist."

Emily shrugged. "More or less. We're all about saving Mother Earth and her creatures."

"Are there many of you locally?"

"Well, there's Tim, Larry, and Drew." She ticked each on off on her fingers. "No wait. Drew moved to Arizona last month."

"There are only three of you?"

"It's not a big organization," she admitted. "Greenpeace thinks we're weirdos and the local covens think we're zealots." She shrugged nonchalantly as if fitting in was low on her list of priorities.

"I take it the Temple of Gaia is less organized than those groups."

"Oh, yeah, for sure."

The waitress returned with pots of tea, plates of scones, jam, and what passed for clotted cream in these parts. Really it was more like over beaten whipped cream.

As we dug in, Emily regaled me with stories of travelling the world to free caged animals, chain herself to trees, and other environmental activities. "It's been a blast," she said through a mouthful of cranberry orange scone. "I mean, I could do it here, but it's more fun to travel."

"And meet other members of the Temple of Gaia, I imagine."

"Yep. That's the best part. I mean, we're pretty scattered, so meeting up is a big deal."

It was sounding less and less like the Temple of Gaia had anything like the organization required for the Sumerian spell. They seemed far more interested in making environmental statements in the natural world than anything supernatural.

After we finished our scones and I paid—it was pretty clear Emily was living hand to mouth—Emily eagerly invited me to a fundraiser in Seattle, which I politely declined. As we went our separate ways, frustration reared its ugly head. It felt like I was getting nowhere fast. Only one more lead and if that didn't pan out, I was stuck.

# # #

The last group on my list was the Daughters of Ishtar. I couldn't see how the followers of a fertility goddess could be behind all this, but I was running out of leads. I had to follow each one, even the weirdest, although I was pretty sure Miles and the Esoteric whatsis had won that award.

I was also running out of time. If Hannah was right, whatever was affecting the Djinn and the Sidhe would eventually hit me, and I couldn't have that. It wasn't just me anymore. I had the peanut to worry about now.

The Daughters of Ishtar were based on the East Coast, so I set up a meeting with their leader, Aris, at a little farmhouse she owned in the New Jersey countryside. I'd never thought of New Jersey having rural areas, but as I stepped from the portal, I realized my mistake. Aris's seventeenth-century farmhouse sat on a very picturesque piece of property surrounded by a split-rail fence nearly as old as the house itself. The rolling green of the lawn was edged in lush bushes and brilliant flowers. Birds chirped in the peaceful afternoon air. It was all so...pastoral.

Aris was waiting for me on the back porch. Her long dark hair, streaked with silver, hung loose down her back, and she wore a flowing, blue cotton dress that covered her feet and swept the floorboards. Thick chunky beads graced her neck. Even from a distance, power radiated off her.

I walked toward her with a friendly smile. "Aris, thank you for meeting with me," I said as I approached. "I could really use your help."

"But of course, Morgan Bailey. Whatever I can do to help a hunter." Was it just me, or was there snark in her tone? It was hard to tell, her expression was so placid, her strange, silver eyes so calm.

"How do you know I'm a hunter?" It wasn't something I went around advertising.

"I have contacts in the SRA. They tell me things. Please," she said with a graceful nod. "Come inside. Let us have a cup of tea, and you can tell me how I may help you and the SRA."

I didn't bother correcting her. The SRA had nothing to do with my current mission. If Trevor knew I was investigating Kabita's death, he'd be pissed off. He'd be happy if he could lock me away until his nephew or niece was born. Good thing he wasn't the boss of me. Well, he sort of was, but not enough to pull that shit.

I followed Aris inside. The kitchen was clearly the oldest part of the house. The ceiling was beamed and low. Anyone taller than my five foot five would be hard-pressed to stand up straight. The floor was made of flagstones, worn smooth from centuries of cooks pacing the room. A huge butcher block took up the center of the room, while more modern appliances and cupboards surrounded the outer walls. The glass in the window above the sink had that wavy thing going on that gave away the fact it was nearly as old as the house. It was a cozy sort of place.

A turquoise kettle whistled on the stove, and Aris rescued it from the burner. She poured hot water into a teapot.

"This is my own concoction. An herbal elixir. Very soothing to the nerves." She gave me a pointed look. "And the stomach."

"Uh, great. Sounds good." I was not a fan of herbal tea, but ever since I got pregnant, everybody seemed to be foisting it on me.

Carrying the teapot to the table, Aris poured the yellowish liquid into two delicate teacups. Mine had pansies on it. Hers, roses. I waited for her to take the first sip before trying mine. I tried really hard not to make a face. It tasted like lawn clippings.

Aris laughed. "I know it's not the best flavor, but trust me, it works."

I took another sip. "If you say so."

She smiled knowingly. "It'll help."

"What? Do I have 'pregnant' tattooed on my forehead?"

This time her laughter was loud and long. "Not at all, but it's sort of a gift of mine, as a healer and a daughter of Ishtar. She was the goddess of fertility, you know."

"So I've heard."

"Now, how is it I can help you?"

I wasn't sure how to broach the subject without accusing a complete stranger of committing murder, so that's what I did. "I want to know if you and the other members of The Daughters of Ishtar are responsible for casting an ancient Sumerian spell that's causing sickness among the supernatural races."

Her eyes widened. "That's quite an accusation."

"Not accusing, just asking."

"Why would you assume we would do such a thing? Because we follow Ishtar?"

"That is a Sumerian connection." I remembered the energy I'd felt from her earlier. "And there's the power. Aren't a lot of people left in this world with the ability to wield such a spell. Maybe you and your, ah, sisters have that ability."

She took another thoughtful sip of her tea, and I followed suit. Surprisingly I was feeling better. Best I'd felt in ages, actually.

"I can see how you would think we may be involved," Aris said at last, "but I assure you, casting such spells is not in our nature, even if we did have access to ancient texts, which we do not. Ishtar was the goddess of fertility, love, and sex. That is what we embrace, not this evil of which you speak."

I sighed and drank more tea. The nausea was indeed retreating, and I was feeling energetic and awake for the first time in three months. "What's in this stuff?"

"Oh, this and that." Aris smiled. "Ginger to calm the stomach, chamomile to soothe the nerves, and peppermint to stimulate. A few other odds and ends. Perfectly safe and very effective."

"I don't suppose I can get some from you?" Maybe Emory could recreate it for me.

Aris's smile widened. "I would be happy to give you a care package. I take it you're satisfied with my innocence."

I sighed. "For the moment." Actually, I wasn't entirely satisfied, but I didn't know how else to get at the truth. Might as well let her think I was satisfied. Maybe she'd slip up. "Thanks for your time."

She smiled. "Anytime, hunter. Anytime."

# # #

I desperately needed to clear my mind. I was out of leads, out of hope, and grief weighed on me like a heavy cloak of smothering darkness. Underneath it all was anger. Anger at whoever had killed Kabita and unleashed this nasty spell, at myself for being unable to figure it out, and at Kabita for being an idiot and dying on me.

The minute I was back through the portal and on my home turf, I geared up and headed out. It wasn't dark yet, but I could at least get set up and ready. Laurelhurst Park wasn't far; in a few minutes, I parked my car on the street next to it.

It was a beautiful park with rolling green lawns, clusters of native trees and shrubs, and crisscrossing walking paths surrounding a small, man-made lake. Well, pond, really. During the day ducks, geese, and swans paddled about, squawking for snacks from passersby. It was nearly deserted, however, the setting sun casting long shadows and the air taking on a chill.

A handful of people still roamed about: a mother herding her three young children away from the playground, a couple strolling hand in hand around the water, and a homeless guy trying to take a nap under a bush. My neck remained firmly unprickled. Not a vampire around.

The Darkness was as grumpy and restless as I was. It snarled and snapped, wanting out, wanting loose. I tamped it down. The last thing I needed was for my power to run wild.

The light faded, taking with it the last warmth of the sun. The couple vacated the park. Mother and children were long gone. Only the homeless guy slept on, unaware and uninterested in the passing of the day.

Something rustled in the bushes, and I froze, calling up a touch of the Darkness to enhance my vision. Something darted out into the open for a split second before scurrying away. Fucking squirrel. Seriously, were there no vampires hanging out in this park at all? This was ridiculous. I could stake it out a bit longer, but I was impatient. There must be somewhere else the vamps were hanging tonight. Not enough prey here, I guessed.

With a sigh of disappointment, I trudged toward the exit. So much for clearing my mind.

Something gripped the back of my neck. My skin prickled with awareness. I wouldn't be disappointed after all.

I turned to face the oncoming vamp. At first it was unaware of me, entirely focused on the sleeping man in his leafy bed. Fangs flashed in the soft glow of the lights lining the path around the pond. The vamp was male, his hair cut short and his jeans worn snug. He was old, maybe a couple of hundred years. His age pressed on me, making me queasy. Not my usual reaction, but thanks to the peanut, this was par for the course these days.

I slid a blade from the sheath along my spine. It was a new design, halfway between a sword and a machete. Tessalah, supernatural weapons expert, had designed it just for me. The hilt fit my hand perfectly. The balance was a glorious thing. The edge was so sharp it could slice paper in half with a flick of my wrist. I remembered the old joke about naming a sword "Kindness" and killing people with it. It was amusing, but I wasn't the sort to name my weapons.

I stalked toward the vamp, blade at the ready. This was so what I needed right now. A smile tugged at my lips, and the Darkness slipped into my eyes, tinging the edges of my vision in purple-black.

I was maybe a hundred yards away when the vamp's head snapped in my direction. He grinned, his fangs looking even bigger and freakier. "Hunter," he hissed. He didn't sound particularly scared. Stupid vampire.

"Hey. Nice evening," I shot back. "You sure your mama gave you permission to be out here all by your lonesome?"

He sneered. "You should be on your way, Hunter. Don't want to lose your head." He laughed wildly at his own joke. Great. All the vampires in Portland, and I had to get a crazy one.

"I'm not worried about that."

"No?"

"Not at all. See, the last vamp who threatened me is so much ash and dust." I rushed him then, flicking my blade so it caught him across the cheek. I'd meant to take his head, but he moved too fast, dammit.

He swung with his fist—unusual for a vamp— and I ducked, and barely missed getting bashed in the head. Another slash, and I cut open a nice hole in his side. He let out an unholy shriek, but it wasn't of pain. He was pissed.

Good. That made two of us.

I whirled to the side as he slashed at me with clawed fingers. His long nails scratched a furrow in my forearm. Stung like a son-of-a-bitch. I smashed him in the nose with the hilt of my blade. Dark, thick blood spurted from his broken appendage. Well, not so much spurted as oozed. He hadn't fed in a while.

"You fucking bitch," he snarled, words slurred by blood and pain. "I'm going to kill you for that."

"Go ahead and try." I called up the Darkness, letting it roar into me, filling me. I knew the moment vamp boy caught on. His eyes widened, and he looked terrified. My eyes must have turned black. Before he could react, I slashed again, cutting deep. He staggered, either from pain or shock—it was hard to tell. His eyes were transfixed on me, and I wondered what he saw there. The Darkness could be scary.

It howled and roared and generally carried on. It wanted to be free, but that wasn't an option. I needed to maintain control lest I become one of the monsters.

It flooded me with power and energy. I forgot all about my queasiness and the pregnancy, and I danced. The blade flashed and I struck time and time again until the world around me became a whirling blur.

"Hey, lady. What kinda dance is that? You in the circus or somethin'?"

I came to myself slowly, the Darkness shrinking back into me. The homeless man had woken and was sitting up in front of his bush, watching me with fascination. "What?"

"You're real good. Wouldn't mind seeing that again."

I stared at the blade in my hand, confused. The water shimmered gently in the lamplight, and moths fluttered around the lamps. Frogs chirped off to my right, and leaves rustled quietly in a gentle breeze. There was no one left in the park but me and the homeless man. Where had the vamp gone?

"You been burnin' something?" the man asked.

"Huh?" Real intelligent. "I mean, what are you talking about?"

He nodded at my feet.

I looked down and saw a pile of ash lying on the path, barely discernable among the pebbles and cracks. I'd dusted him, and I hadn't even known it.

Chapter 16

The hunt didn't help. I was still edgy, unfocused, bubbling with rage. In fact, I was making myself sick. Peanut didn't like mommy all worked up.

The minute I got home, I made myself a cup of tea using the weeds Aris had given me. It smelled weird, but a few sips in, I was calmer and less queasy.

Inigo found me an hour later, still sitting at the dining room table, basking in the glow of feeling halfway normal. An hour without feeling like hurling is, believe me, a gift of the gods.

"Hello, love." He kissed the top of my head. It wasn't what I wanted. I stood up so quickly, my chair hit the floor with a crash. I ignored it, grabbed his neck, and pulled him down for a crushing kiss.

I felt his astonishment as he hesitated, but it only lasted a split second. His tongue swept inside to tangle with mine, igniting me. I moaned, writhing against him like a wanton thing. He grabbed my ass, pulling me hard against him until I could feel his thick shaft pressing against my belly. I groaned aloud. I wanted him. Bad.

I ripped at his T-shirt, trying to get it over his head. He helped me, his breath coming in quick little pants as I struggled to unbutton his jeans.

"Jesus, Morgan," he moaned. "What's gotten into you? Not that I'm complaining—"

"Shut up," I ordered. "I need you now."

He tore my clothes off, scattering them around the kitchen. The scent of our arousal was heady. My body was slick with need. I wrapped one hand around his thick length, and he gasped.

He slid a finger into me, making a sound of pleasure as I clenched around him. "Gods, you're so ready."

"Now. Take me now." I was going to lose my mind if he didn't hurry this up.

He laid me down on our pile of clothing, right there in the middle of the kitchen. He positioned himself, and with a groan, buried himself to the hilt.

I arched toward him, crying out as every nerve ending screamed in bliss. It had been way too long since we'd done this. I pulled him closer, wordlessly begging for more, urging him to go deeper, faster.

He buried his face against my shoulder and thrust into me over and over until we were both panting and cursing, straining for that final edge.

Our movements grew frenzied. Pleasure wound tighter and tighter in my belly.

And then it burst, and the edge rushed to meet me.

Chapter 17

"What the hell did you do to me?"

There was a long pause on the other end of the line, then Aris said, "What do you mean?" Her tone was calm with only the slightest hint of curiosity.

"That damn tea."

"Could you be more specific? Did you have some sort of reaction?"

"I'll say." I paced the kitchen, practically snarling in outrage. "It made me..." Okay, this was awkward, telling a complete stranger. I barreled on. "It made me horny." I could feel my cheeks flaming. I wasn't a prude—far from it—but this was a situation in which I'd never found myself before. I was distinctly uncomfortable.

"Ah. That."

"Yeah. That. What the fuck, Aris?"

"I apologize. I should have warned you." She sounded amused, which pissed me off even more.

"You knew about this?" I screeched.

"Well, it is a known side effect, but it's fairly rare. And most people appreciate it."

"Well, I am not most people," I snapped.

"Clearly."

I literally snarled.

"I do apologize, Morgan. I should have warned you."

"Yes, yes you should have." I paused a beat. "Do you have any more?"

She laughed.

I hung up a few minutes later, after she'd promised to pop some more tea in the mail. I felt like a gullible idiot, but frankly, I was feeling the best I had in months. Well, the last couple months anyway. My mother insisted the morning sickness would pass, but it was more like all-day sickness, and it definitely wasn't passing. If anything it was getting worse. If I had to drink some gross ass tea to feel better, and it had the rather awkward side effect of me wanting to get it on with my boyfriend every five minutes, so be it.

The downside was I still wasn't sure Aris and her group of merry witches wasn't behind the spell and Kabita's death. I needed to feel better about that. Drinking tea from a possible killer was probably a bad idea.

I dialed Eddie at the shop. He picked up on the third ring.

"Majicks and Potions," he said cheerfully.

"Hey, Eddie. I need some info."

"If I have it, it's yours."

"Have you ever heard of the Daughters of Ishtar?"

"Can't say I have."

I sank down at the kitchen table. "They're a coven of witches who follow Ishtar. She was the Sumerian goddess of fertility."

"And war."

I blinked. "What?"

"Ishtar was the goddess of love and fertility in ancient Sumeria, but she was also the goddess of war."

"Thanks, Eddie."

I barely heard his response as I hung up. Aris and her people worshipped a war goddess. How had I missed that? And what was more an act of war than the murder of a demon hunter and an attack on the supernatural races.

I was pretty sure I'd found the guilty parties. Dammit. And I really liked their tea.

Shéa MacLeod

Chapter 18

The front door of the farmhouse crashed inward. Wood exploded into splinters everywhere. Men shouted, heavy boots thudding across creaky wooden floors.

I followed the chaos inside, making my way into the familiar kitchen. It was empty, like the rest of the house.

"Was this necessary?" I snapped at Trevor. When I'd called him with my suspicions, he'd dragged one of his SRA teams along with him on the "raid."

"I thought you wanted these people caught."

"Yes. Caught, not shot in the head or beat to death. For fuck's sake, keep your men under control." They were ripping open cupboard doors and flinging things around. Something crashed overhead, and I winced. "Seriously? Your men are assholes."

"They're just doing their job." I gave him a look. He sighed heavily but turned to an armed men standing near him. "Order a stand-down. The place is empty."

The man trotted of, muttering into his radio. I breathed easier. Aris and her followers may worship a war goddess, and they might be guilty of practicing some seriously nasty magic, but I couldn't condone this sort of behavior from what were effectively the police of the supernatural world. Granted, I'd have done the same with a nest of vamps, but that was another matter.

"They must have caught wind of us coming," Trevor mused.

"I don't see how," I said. I stared out over the large garden. Green leaves rustled lightly in the breeze. The weather vane on top the small red barn pointed west. A flash of something caught my attention. "Barn."

"What?"

I gave him a hard look. "Your men follow my lead, got it?"

He crossed his arms. "Excuse me?"

"Since they can't control themselves, I'm going to have to control them." I crossed my arms, too, shooting him a glare. I had expected better from him and his men.

He sighed. "Whatever. If you think you can bring them in."

"I know I can."

He issued terse orders through his radio. "Okay, you're good to go."

I let myself out the back door. The grass beneath my feet was soft and springy and smelled newly mown. A bee buzzed lazily over my head before zipping off on its own business. Beneath it all hummed an odd energy I couldn't quite place. It itched beneath my skin like tiny bugs. I made a valiant attempt not to squirm.

Cautiously I pulled open the barn door and slipped inside. It was almost pitch black, and I could just make out the huddled shapes of farm equipment. The scent of dried mud and old hay tickled my nose. Trevor's men pounded across the lawn. So much for behaving themselves.

The explosion tossed me off my feet. I tumbled into a hay bale, coughing from the cloud of smoke. Lights flashed in front of my eyes, and there was shouting and chaos.

I stumbled to my feet, swaying almost like I was drunk. My vision was blurry, and my head spun, whether from the impact or the sweet scent of the smoke, I wasn't sure. Someone grabbed my arm, and the Darkness roared to life. Without a thought, I threw him off. The SRA agent tumbled head over teakettle out the barn door.

Everything was clear now. Tinged with purple, but clear. I marched through the cloud of smoke and the confused agents right up to a small back door I hadn't noticed before. I threw it open in time to see a cluster of women headed for the trees. I ran.

The Darkness ran before me, wrapping tendrils of inky, purplish-black around the ankles of the fleeing women, dragging them to the ground. I was on Aris in a moment, tendrils of Darkness wrapping around her waist, squeezing the breath from her body.

"Mercy," she gasped.

"What? Like you gave the Sidhe? The Djinn? The dragons?" Rage engulfed me. "Kabita?"

"I d-don't know what you're talking about." Her face was turning red as she struggled to breathe. I snapped at the Darkness, and it let her go. By then the agents had recovered and were handcuffing the Daughters of Ishtar. I focused on Aris, their leader.

"Seriously? You're going to play that card? You lied to me, Aris."

"I didn't—"

"We know what you're up to," Trevor interjected.

Aris blanched. I could see her internal struggle. Now we were getting somewhere. She was going to confess.

"We only did it once," she blurted.

I narrowed my eyes. "Don't you think once was enough? They're dying, Aris. And the rest of us will, too, thanks to your greed."

She blinked. "Greed?"

"For power." I wanted to add "duh," but that would have been ridiculously immature.

Her eyes widened. "You're after us for the Sumerian spell thing?"

This time I did say it. "Duh."

"No. No." She shook her head. "We thought you were after us for—"

"The necromancy," one of the older women blurted. She was sitting on the ground in a grass-stained white robe, her white hair a nimbus around her head.

"Necromancy?" I parroted, completely confused.

"Raising people from the dead is illegal," Trevor said grimly.

"Oh, not people," Aris assured us. "Cats, or rather one cat."

Trevor and I stared at her, then we turned to each other. He was clearly as confused as I was. "Cats?" we said at the same time.

"Marion lost her cat recently." Aris nodded to the woman with the white hair. "She was devastated. So we decided to try and bring it back." She shrugged. "It worked. But we knew necromancy was illegal, so we had to hide what we did."

I groaned. "And that's why you ran. Because you thought the SRA was here to arrest you for necromancy."

She shrugged again.

"Oh, for fuck's sake," Trevor snapped. "We don't give a crap about necromancing cats. You can raise an entire cemetery of pets if you want. All we care about is that you don't raise humans from the dead."

"We'd never dream of it," Aris assured us. The rest of the Daughters of Ishtar murmured their agreement.

After that there was a lot of apologizing and handcuff unlocking and general embarrassment. I think Trevor might have been a little irritated at me, but I ignored him. I'd had legitimate reasons to suspect Aris and the Daughters of Ishtar of casting the Sumerian spell.

"I'm really sorry about all this," I said awkwardly.

"And I'm sorry about throwing the smoke bomb at you." Aris offered me a small smile. "Got time for tea?"

"Why not?

I should have been out hunting Kabita's killer, but my best suspects had just been eliminated. Tea sounded like a damned good idea.

# # #

"What are you going to do now?" Inigo asked.

We were drinking coffee the next morning at the kitchen table. Regular for him, decaf for me.

I sighed. "The only thing I can do. Take a deeper look into the local coven. I don't know what else I can do. I've got no other suspects."

"What about the Esoteric Divine Worshippers of Ra?"

"I spoke to Vane earlier. They haven't got any magic at all. Even if they wanted to cast such a spell, they couldn't. And I don't see what a spell like that would gain them." I buried my face in my hands. "This is so aggravating."

He stood up and walked behind me and began rubbing my shoulders. I nearly groaned with delight. "You're too tense, love. You need to relax."

"I'll relax when Kabita's killer is behind bars, not before."

He placed a gentle kiss on top my head. "Why does that not surprise me?"

"Well, it shouldn't. You've known me long enough."

"I'm going with you."

"If you want." I didn't need him. I could do it on my own, but I didn't want to hurt his feelings or start another argument. Besides, having him along would be nice.

"I want."

"As soon as we finish breakfast, I'm going over to that church to meet with Hannah. They're having a get-together there this morning."

"How do you know?"

"I read it on their website."

He laughed. "Of course you did."

As soon as we finished our breakfast, we drove over to the church. The same dozen or so coven members were there, gathered in a room off the kitchen on the most uncomfortable looking folding chairs. They were chatting animatedly. There was zero magic going on, but I sensed mild power from a few of them.

"Morgan!" Hannah jumped up from her seat, a startled expression on her face. As before, she was perfectly coiffed and dressed in black slacks, a cream silk shell, and a red tailored jacket. Her gold jewelry was expensive and understated. Her cosmetics were expensive and flawless. "What a surprise." She sounded pleased to see me, which I wouldn't have expected of someone guilty of murder. Then again, maybe she was a really good actress.

"This is Inigo." They shook hands politely. "I need to talk to you," I said, trying to keep my voice low. It was no use. The other members of the group instantly perked up their ears. They pretended not to listen, but it was pretty clear I was the center of attention.

"Maybe we should do this outside," Inigo murmured.

"Whatever you have to say to me, you can say in front of us all." Hannah folded her hands neatly in front of her. There were zero signs of guilt or fear, only calm.

"The Sumerian spell is still a problem."

She frowned, a tiny line appearing between her eyebrows. "The one we spoke of on your last visit? I wish I could help, but—"

"I know you're involved." I knew no such thing, but sometimes confrontation forces out truth.

Hannah stared at me a moment, her face a mask of surprise. Not the "oh no, you caught me" sort of surprise, but more the "what the fuck?" kind. "That's impossible."

"Nothing is impossible."

"No, you don't understand." She glanced at her fellow coven members. They all exhibited various levels of astonishment. "We *can't* mess with a spell like that. It literally isn't possible. It's against our nature to harm anyone, and that is certainly a harmful spell."

"And I'm supposed to take your word for it?"

She'd opened her mouth to respond when there was a commotion at the front of the church. Two brawny men hauled in a much thinner man. In fact, he was downright skinny and had wild, graying hair and a skeevy beard that hit mid-chest. His jeans hung off narrow hips, and he wore a carved wooden charm on a leather cord around his neck. His green T-shirt had a pot leaf on the front, and the odor wafting off him matched it.

"What's going on?" Hannah snapped. "Karl?"

The man on the right shook the skinny pothead. "He's been stripped, Hannah."

Her eyes widened, and there were horrified gasps from the other members. "Are you certain?" she whispered.

"What's going on?" I interrupted. "What do you mean, he's been stripped?" He looked clothed to me.

The man called Karl ignored me, focused on Hannah. "Absolutely sure. He hasn't got an ounce of magic left."

Hannah tentatively touched the pothead's cheek. She flinched as if she'd scalded herself. "Oh, Dom," she whispered. "What did you do?"

"I didn't mean to," the pothead whined.

Karl gave him a shake. "Tell her what you did, Dom."

Dom whined some more but finally blurted, "They were eating my plants, man. I had to stop them, or I'd have lost my whole crop."

Hannah closed her eyes as if in pain. "What. Did. You. Do?" She bit out each word, anger thrumming in her voice.

Dom tried to extricate himself from Karl and his beefy buddy, and finally gave up. He wilted. "I put up electric fences, but I must have set the juice too high."

"He killed a deer." Karl's tone was flat.

Hannah opened her eyes. "Oh, Dom."

"I didn't meant to." He was crying now, tears running down his thin, weathered face.

She stepped back and gave him a stern look. "Dominic Melton, I hereby banish you from this coven forever." She pointed to the exit. "Go."

Karl and the other beefy guy let go of Dom. Without a word, the pothead slunk out of the church. He looked back just once, sorrow etched on his face.

"You see," Hanna said at last, eyes shining with unshed tears. "That is why we couldn't have done that thing. That awful spell."

"Sorry, I don't get it." What did a banished pothead have to do with a spell?

Her expression was grim. "My great-aunt started this coven nearly forty years ago. She was a very powerful witch, and she wanted to ensure that anyone who chose to join our coven had to follow the tenets of our faith. She cast a spell. Any of our members who have sworn their allegiance are barred from harming any living creature."

"If they do?" I asked, already knowing the answer.

"The spell my aunt cast will strip them of all their powers, and we will be forced to banish them."

Holy shit. "Even if it's an accident."

"Unfortunately, yes. Our members know what they're agreeing to when they join, and most of them are quite serious about it. However, now and again accidents do happen. You see the result." She gazed at the front of the church where Dom had disappeared.

"You didn't cast the spell," I said lamely.

"No. We couldn't have cast that spell even if we'd wanted to."

# # #

I was interrupted by a knock on the kitchen door. It was my brother, Trevor. His expression was grim as I ushered him inside. Well, grimmer than usual. Trevor wasn't exactly know for merriment.

"What's up, Trev?"

"I've got the results of Kabita's autopsy."

I was going to need something strong for this. Unfortunately, the peanut meant no alcohol. No real coffee either. Decaf wasn't going to do it, so I rummaged around the cupboards and found some hot chocolate. I waggled the tin in the air. "Want some?"

He frowned. "Not really. I don't suppose you have something stronger?"

I sighed and snagged a bottle of whisky from the same cupboard. Not my cuppa, but Inigo liked it. It made him nostalgic.

I busied myself making hot chocolate and pouring his whisky. Maybe I was putting things off. Okay, I totally was, but sometimes having answers was worse than not having them.

Finally I set both mugs on the table and sat down across from him. I took a fortifying sip of cocoa. "Okay, spill it."

"Kabita was burned out."

"How can you even tell that?"

"I don't mean tired." He glanced at me over the rim of his mug. "I mean, magically. She was drained completely of her power."

I frowned. That sometimes happened to me when I used the Darkness too much. "How could that have killed her?"

He set his mug down carefully and leaned forward, propping his elbows on the table in a way that would have given my mother fits. "They didn't drain her, Morgan. They burned her out. Burned her up. Used every ounce of magic in her down to a molecular scale."

"They?" I felt numb.

"This is not something that happens in the natural order of things. Someone did this to her. Someone used her for her magic to fuel...something."

"Like a spell," I said stiffly. I had a bad feeling I knew now what had happened.

"That's the most common reason, yes. If a practitioner doesn't have enough magic of her own, she can tap into someone else's to fuel the spell."

"Why Kabita?"

He leaned back thoughtfully. "Kabita was a very powerful witch and a hunter. She would have had a lot of magic. She could have powered a very big spell."

Like the ancient Sumerian one that was killing the supernatural races. "Why would Kabita have done that? Why would she have helped them with a spell so awful? Especially knowing it would eventually kill her friends?"

"She wouldn't have."

I blinked. "Are you telling me she was forced?"

"It's the only likely scenario."

"They killed her to fuel their damn spell." My voice was low, dangerous.

"Yes."

Fury built in me like a living thing. "Who would do such a thing?"

"I was hoping that was something you could find out."

Chapter 19

I dialed Vane's number. He picked up immediately.

"I need more information on this spell," I blurted.

"The Sumerian thing?" He coughed a little. It sounded phlegmy.

"Yeah. Are you getting sick?"

There was a pause. "Let us just say it would behoove us to solve this as quickly as possible. I don't know how much more I can give you, but go ahead."

Great. Now Vane was being affected by the spell. This didn't bode well. I gave him a rundown of what Trevor had told me about Kabita being magically burned out. "What does that mean for the spell? I mean, would somebody do that? Could they do that?"

There was a long pause, during which I heard him turning pages. "I believe it is possible, yes. There's another spell, also Sumerian. It binds a person to a second spell in order to boost power to that spell. You can use it on one person or several, depending on the power needed. Like linking up car batteries."

Holy shit. Holy fucking shit. "How many?"

"How many what?"

"How many people could you link?"

"As many as you needed, as long as you have a focus point."

"A focus point being a person?"

"Exactly. One main person, then you link the others through that person so their energies flow through him or her. A conduit, if you will."

I tried to steady my breath. I was starting to hyperventilate. "What would happen to the focus, the conduit, after the spell was done?"

"Likely nothing unless the spellcaster used too much power. Then you might fry their power. Temporarily anyway." Another pause. "How many people are we talking about?"

"Thousands."

"Excuse me?"

"Thousands. Not human, either, but supernatural races. What would happen if you tried to drain the power of thousands of supernaturals through one conduit?"

"Fuck."

I closed my eyes against the image in my head.

"Who would need that kind of power?" he asked. "And why? I mean, that is an incredible amount of power."

I had a very bad idea I knew the answer to the first. The second? Well, we'd just see about that.

Chapter 20

The portal let me out in the middle of a grassy field. A confused cow stared at me a moment before returning to its cow business. A narrow track, beaten down by centuries of foot traffic, stretched across the pasture. To the right, it disappeared into a thicket of trees. To the left, it curved out of sight around a briar patch.

I pulled out my smartphone and used its map app to orient myself. To the left it was.

As I rounded the briars, a sweeping vista came into view. The hill curved gently downward into a lush valley. In the very center was a small village and beyond, the hills rose again, blue-tinged against the setting sun.

I tromped down the path, my boots thudding heavily with each step. I was tired, and I didn't want to do this. I wanted to be at home, drinking hot chocolate and soaking in a giant tub. Better yet would be wine, but that wasn't happening. Not for ages yet. I missed wine. And coffee. But at least I had an excuse to eat donuts. If they didn't make me sick.

"Focus, Morgan," I muttered. "Don't lose your shit now." Because that would be awkward.

As I drew near the village, I spotted the pub. I envisioned its warm coziness and dreaded this confrontation more than ever.

Inside, the pub was exactly as I remembered it: low beamed ceilings, a fire dancing cheerfully on the ancient hearth, bottles glowing beneath the lights above the back shelf of the bar. A couple of regulars sat there, hunched over their pints. The one in the cranberry-colored sweater with the hole in the left elbow was regaling the one with the muddy boots with a tale of some long ago fishing trip. In a corner next to the fire, a couple of tourists sipped glasses of wine and studied a guidebook while arguing about what they would explore the next day. It was all so homey and innocent.

"Hi, Miles." I leaned on the bar and caught the barman's eye.

Miles blanched but recovered quickly. "Why, Miss Bailey. How lovely to see you. I thought you returned home to America. Bill, Stanley, did you know Miss Bailey comes from America? Somewhere north of Los Angeles, I believe." He glanced at me for affirmation, which I gave him with a barely restrained eye roll. Why was it that the entire rest of the world seemed unaware anything existed between LA and Seattle? And the only reason they knew Seattle was that Meg Ryan movie.

"We need to talk, Miles."

"Sure, sure," he said, swiping at the bar with a soggy towel. "How may I help you?"

"I mean in private."

"Sorry, love. No one to watch the bar. Go ahead and talk. Don't mind Bill and Stanley. They pretty much live here."

The other two nodded and made encouraging sounds. I sighed. This wasn't going to go well.

"Remember that thing we talked about last time I was here?"

He mulled it over, looking confused. Then his brow unwrinkled. "Ah, yes. The curse."

"Spell."

Bill and Stanley stared at me with wide eyes.

"She's looking for someone who used some sort of ancient spell," Miles explained to the men. "Egyptian was it?"

"Sumerian."

"Ah, right. Sumerian."

Bill, the one in the holey sweater, scrunched up his nose and rubbed his cheekbone. "Around here? Who would be into that sort of thing? Ain't done now, is it?"

"Nope." Stanley, the more laconic of the two, shook his head. "Ain't done."

"See? There you have it. It's just not something we'd mess about with." Miles gave me what I assumed was supposed to be a charming smile. Instead he looked constipated.

"So the Esoteric Divine Worshippers of Ra would never cast such a spell? Under any circumstances?"

"Can't see why they would."

"What if they did it behind your back because they knew you wouldn't approve?"

He winced. "Can't see why they'd do that either. What would be the purpose?"

That was a very good question, so I answered with my own. "Isn't it true the members of your group have very little power of their own?"

He looked embarrassed. "We don't like to discuss such things. We strive to better ourselves through meditation and ritual practice." It sounded like he was quoting a brochure.

I rested one butt cheek on a stool. "But what if there were a shortcut?"

He turned pale then. "I don't know what you mean."

"It was clear to me at our last meeting that, while you yourself have little to no power, you wished very much to have more."

"Who doesn't?" Bill chuckled. "Them politicians down in London are always trying for it."

I ignored him. "I'm guessing that many of your followers feel the same. They'd give just about anything for the kind of power the witchblood wield naturally."

Miles shrugged. "So? Who can blame them? It's easy enough for those with power to take it for granted. Imagine having none." He gave me a pointed look.

"Fair enough. And I applaud you trying to better yourself. However, what I can't condone is the way you went about it."

His chin went up. "I don't know what you mean."

I leaned forward, infringing on his personal space, something I knew most Brits were uncomfortable with. "Yes, you do. You know exactly what I'm talking about." Aris and her group were already powerful, as was the local coven. The Temple of Gaia had neither the numbers, nor the interest. Only Miles's group had both the membership and the desire that would lead them to attempt such a horrible spell.

A rough hand grabbed my arm and yanked me away from the stool and the bar. "That's quite enough, Missy." It was Bill of the holey sweater.

"Get. Your. Hands. Off. Me." I bit out each word, fury cracking through me.

"I don't think so," Bill said. "We don't need your kind poking your noses in our business."

"Bill, this isn't necessary." Miles's voice was shaking, which made me more than a little nervous.

"Shut your hole, Miles." Bill didn't even glance at the other man. "I've had enough of your whinging. It's time someone with stones took the lead."

"And I suppose that's you, is it?" I snarled.

"You're about to find out."

Bill dragged me outside into the gravel parking lot. It had started to rain, and the drizzle hung in the air like a fine curtain. Overhead, dark clouds boiled like a bad omen.

"Why?" I asked.

"Right on the money, love." His tone was cocky and condescending. "Most of us were tired of Miles and his fake bullshit. We wanted the real thing. Real magic. Real power."

"So you decided to steal it?"

"Gotta do what you gotta do."

"I don't get it. You'd need power to cast the spell in the first place."

He gave me a smug look. "My mother was a witch. My sister inherited some of her power. She agreed to help us even though she's not a member of our group. After that, it was easy enough to lure someone with the real power we needed for our spell."

"By faking a rogue dragon, roaming the streets of Liverpool?"

He grinned. "I know my audience, and I had to get her out from under MI8."

"But why Liverpool?"

He seemed to think it over. "We like it over there. Good place to cast a spell." And dump a body where no one would connect it to them. I could almost hear that thought rattling around in his stupid brain.

"What about the attack at Kabita's funeral. Was that you?"

"Sorry about that." He didn't sound sorry. "But you were getting too close." Little did he know I'd been flailing in the dark.

Gods, I wanted to rip his eyes out. "Did you know you'd kill Kabita with the spell?"

His silence was all the confession I needed. The Darkness was howling now, wanting out. My fury was feeding it, and I didn't care.

"How about the Djinn and the Sidhe? The dragons? Did you know the spell would kill them?"

"Now that was a surprise. We were only going to drain some of their power. Share the wealth and all that." It was clear he didn't care what happened to the other races as long as he got what he wanted.

"And did you know that eventually the spell will kill anyone with an ounce of supernatural blood or magical ability?"

"Long as it doesn't kill me and mine."

His attitude made me even more furious, if that were possible. It was that sort of narcissistic arrogance that wreaked havoc in the world. I was going to stop this bastard if it was the last thing I did.

Bill pulled me across the parking lot, my boots scuffing in the gravel. On the other side lay the field I'd walked across earlier, but now about a dozen people had replaced the cows. They stood there in ridiculous cloaks with hoods. Seriously, these people had been watching way too much TV. Although a hood would have been nice right about now, what with the rain getting in my eyes.

"My fellow worshippers of Ra." Bill's voice boomed as we joined the cloaked figures. "It's time for our next spellworking. We'll use this one as fuel." He shook me by the collar hard enough to rattle teeth.

"Is she strong enough?" one of the shorter figures asked.

"She's a hunter."

There was excited murmuring among the throng. Apparently that was good enough for them. They quickly formed a circle around me and Bill and began chanting in what I assumed was ancient Sumerian. Meanwhile, Bill stripped off his belt and lashed my hands together behind my back. If he thought that would hold me, he was an idiot.

He stepped back and took his place in the circle. The morons hadn't even bothered to cast a protection circle. Gods, it was like letting a two-year-old play with a gun. The sheer stupidity was mind-blowing. These jackasses had to be stopped.

I struggled against the belt around my wrists, but Bill knew what he was doing. There wasn't a fraction of give.

"Why is she smiling?" someone asked.

"Shut up and chant," Bill snapped.

My grin broadened. Imbeciles. I let the Darkness out to play.

Chapter 21

The Darkness rushed out of me in a cloud of purplish black. Usually I was the only one who could see it, but I could tell from the looks on their faces the rest of them could see it, too. I grinned.

The Darkness lashed out, sending a couple of the cloaked figures toppling over onto the wet grass. I wanted to cheer, but I was still tied up. So while everyone else was focused on my sentient powers, I focused on getting free.

I managed to work my wrists together so I could press the release on my wrist cuff. It looked like an ordinary cuff bracelet, but it was one of Tessalah's bits of magic. Inside was a small, deadly blade. Press the catch and out it sprang. With the blade free, I managed to use the fingers of one hand to push the cuff down so the blade could cut through the belt.

The Darkness was having a good time slapping around the members of the Divine Esoteric Worshippers of Ra. What a ridiculous name.

I finally cut through the leather and freed my hands, then snapped the blade back into the cuff. Didn't want to slice open my own veins. Wouldn't need the Ra people to drain me then.

"She's free!" someone yelled. Two burly men rushed toward me, cloaks flapping, sending droplets of moisture everywhere.

I managed to dodge the first one but the second was faster, wilier. He grabbed me, his meaty hand bruising my arm as sausage fingers dug into soft flesh. I kicked him hard in the shin with the toe of my boot. He grunted but didn't let go.

I willed the Darkness to help me, and it did, wrapping itself around my captor's face, effectively smothering him. The man finally let go of my arm and fell to the ground, struggling in vain to tear the Darkness away. He was either unconscious or dead— it was hard to tell. I was hoping for the former. Killing humans—even idiots who messed with things they shouldn't—was not something I did. Killing monsters was bad enough.

Another two figures headed my way. There were too many. Even with the Darkness, there was no way I could stop them all. I didn't know how much power they'd stolen from the Djinn and Sidhe, but if they knew how to use it, things were going to get ugly.

"Dammit, Inigo," I muttered, bracing myself for another attack. "You were right. I should have brought you along."

You called, love?

I jerked my head up, startled. A dragon's cry echoed overhead, and a blue dragon the size of a horse swooped down over the heads of the Ra worshippers. A couple of them took off, terrified by coming face-to-face with a dragon. They didn't get far. Men in black suits were pouring down the hill. Trevor's people.

I brought the cavalry.

Yep. I should probably listen to Inigo more often. I blew him a kiss and waded back in, only to find the Divine Worshippers already on their knees, hands raised. I guess a fire-breathing dragon sort of takes the wind out of your sails.

The pub door swung open, and Trevor stomped out, dragging Miles along with him. As he drew close, he shook his head. "You sure know how to throw a party, Morgan."

"Just warming them up for you," I said. I didn't want to admit how relieved I was to see them. Maybe if I'd still had all those powers, I could have done it on my own. As it was, I was going to have to learn I was stronger with my team than I was alone. I hid a grimace. It was not a comfortable lesson to learn for someone as fiercely independent as me.

"I'm sorry. I'm sorry. We didn't mean to," Miles was babbling.

I didn't buy it for a second. Maybe it wasn't what Miles had wanted, but he'd gone along with it. No doubt Bill had spearheaded the whole thing. He glared at me from where he knelt on the soggy ground. If looks could kill.

"How do we fix this?" I asked my brother. "How do we send the power back to the people they stole it from?"

"You better ask him."

He waved someone forward, and Vane stepped out of the sea of black suits. He held up a sheaf of paper. "I worked out a reverse spell. It won't be comfortable for them"—he nodded at the assholes kneeling on the ground—"but it should work."

"I don't give a damn if they're uncomfortable. It's the least they deserve for what they did."

He nodded. "No time like the present then."

Vane waved, and Jade appeared from the mass of SRA agents. I wasn't sure how I felt about her being there, but hey, if Vane wanted to work with her, who was I to disagree?

Jade was clutching a small, cast-iron pot. It wasn't exactly a witch's cauldron, but it was close. I was pretty sure the thing was a Dutch oven. Inside it were some herbs and bottles and whatnot. She knelt next to Vane in the middle of the circle and pulled things out of the pot. Once it was empty, and the items laid out neatly, Jade selected a large bag of salt. She stood and walked the circle, chanting quietly and scattering salt, not just around the outside of the circle, but within it, as well, consecrating the ground we stood on.

When she finished that, she took pieces of pale wood—ash maybe—and built a small fire. She hung the pot over the fire and poured in a bottle of water. The she gave Vane a nod.

The Dragon King's assassin whipped out the biggest damn knife I'd ever seen. Bill whimpered as Vane approached him. I would have, too. Dude was scary. But Vane didn't slice his throat or any other appendage. Instead he neatly and efficiently cut off a lock of hair, then dumped the clippings in the pot and moved to the next member of the Esoteric Divine Worshippers of Ra. He repeated the process until he'd collected hair clippings from them all.

Jade added what looked like mistletoe to the clippings. You know, the stuff that was hung at Christmas so people kissed each other. Spellcasting was weird. What was even weirder was I hadn't known Jade was a witch. But she'd have to be to perform a ritual this powerful.

Vane joined Jade at the pot, and they held hands over it, chanting in unison. I literally felt the power of the spell building between the two of them. Then, without warning, it spilled out, swirling around the circle, encircling each of the Esoteric people. The spell dove into them like tendrils of an invisible Cthulhu creature, burying itself into the chests of those who'd cast that horrible spell.

I could almost see the power being ripped from them, like a giant hand was pulling fistfuls of cotton from rag dolls. They jerked and toppled as swirls of energy exploded outward from their bodies, flew around the circle, and disappeared into the ether. I had no doubt the power was back where it belonged.

And me? I sat there on the damp grass and cried. I cried for myself. I cried for Kabita. I cried at the feeling of loss that threatened to overwhelm me. I cried until there was nothing left, and then I sat there in a salt-sprinkled field in England until someone lifted me and carried me home.

# # #

That night Kabita appeared to me again, but this time she looked normal—well, as normal as a ghost can look. At least she wasn't trying to kill me.

Sorry. She gave me one of her wry looks.

"It's all good. You okay now?"

For being dead, sure.

My throat swelled, and I suddenly found it hard to breathe. "Why didn't you tell me what was going on? I could have helped."

She looked at my abdomen. *Too dangerous.*

"I wish everyone would stop treating me like an invalid." I was trying really hard not to think about how strange it was, talking to a ghost. The ghost of my best friend. I swiped angrily at my eyes. "If I could get my hands on those bastards that did this to you..." As it was, Trevor had hustled them off and wouldn't let me near them. Probably for the best.

Forgive.

"Easy for you to say. You're not the one that has to live with this." I winced at my word choice. I kept forgetting she was dead.

She grinned. *Not dead. Different.*

"So, what's on the other side?"

Can't tell you. Surprise.

I growled. She laughed, then looked behind her. *Gotta go.*

"Wait..."

She winked. *See ya around.* And then she vanished.

Inigo rolled over and peered at me in the dark. "You talking to someone?"

"Kabita's ghost. She's gone now."

"Ah." He took my hand. "You okay?"

"I'm angry. I mean, I get that these people wanted power. Who doesn't? But to steal it from someone else to the point of draining them of life?" I shook my head. "Prison is too good for them."

"Don't worry. Trevor is a creative guy. Bet they think twice before doing anything like that again."

I had my doubts. "I need to go to the Otherworld tomorrow. Visit the Sidhe, then the Djinn. I need to make sure they're okay." Vane had already assured me the dragons were well on their way to recovery.

He nodded. "I'll go with you."

"You don't have to. I don't need..."

He gave me a stern look. "We're a team, remember? I know you don't need, but maybe I do."

That shut me up. "Okay. Tomorrow, field trip."

He nodded happily. "Good." He rolled over and went back to sleep.

It took me a long time to follow him into dreamland.

Chapter 22

Turned out breaking up the Esoteric Divine Worshippers of Ra and reversing the spell worked like a charm. Kalen and his people were back to normal, as were the Marid and the Djinn. Hopefully nobody else would be getting sick and dying from the power drain.

Trevor and his men had found ancient scrolls in Bill's cottage. I'm not sure what they did with them, but I hope they burned them.

The SRA declared Haakon permanent head of the private investigation firm that was our front, which technically made him my boss. However, I think we reached an understanding that nobody bossed me, no matter how senior he was. Haakon was okay with that. I think he said something about me being a pain in the ass.

Vane took off, back to the Highlands of Scotland and his king, but I had a feeling we'd be seeing him again. There was something in his eyes when he said goodbye.

As for me and Inigo, well, he took me to my first ultrasound appointment. I laid on that sticky vinyl table with my shirt hiked up to my boobs while the technician squeezed cold gel on my bare stomach. I was not amused, but when I heard that tiny heartbeat, I forgot everything else.

"Looking good," the woman said with a motherly smile.

"What is it?" I asked.

"Too early to tell. Be a month or so yet at least." Her eyes widened. "What the...?" She squinted at the monitor. "That's something I've never seen. Must be something wrong with the machine. I'll be right back with a new one." She quickly exited the room, and as her footsteps disappeared down the hall, I leaned forward and stared at the monitor.

There, for the world to see, was a tiny little dragon the size of a plum. It lifted a clawed hand, and I swear to gods, it waved at me.

Inigo laughed all the way home.

Want to read more about Emory Chastain and her coven? Check out this sample of Sunwalker Saga: Witchblood Series: Book 1, Spellwalker

Spellwalker
Sunwalker Saga: Witch Blood
Book One

Chapter 1

"I need a love potion."

The woman on the other side of the counter glared at Emory belligerently, her lower jaw thrust forward. Her skinny body was swathed in a massive fake fur coat despite the warmth of an early summer morning, and her mousy brown hair was scraped back into a tight bun on top of her head. Her muddy eyes snapped in anger, as if Emory had somehow personally affronted her.

Emory Chastain was used to working with challenging customers. She gave the woman a placating smile. "I'm sorry. We don't carry love potions." She picked up a small, brown bottle. "I have a nice herbal tincture for relaxation and stress relief." It wasn't the first time she'd been asked such a bizarre question, and it likely wouldn't be the last. Apparently people thought herbs equaled magical fixes. If only they knew.

"I don't need relaxation," the customer snapped. "I need a love potion. I was told you do that kind of thing."

Emory carefully blanked her face. Who had this woman been talking to? "Do what kind of thing?"

The woman let out a huff of annoyance and edged a little closer. "Magic."

Emory gave a light laugh, but it was forced. "There's no such thing as magic," she said softly.

"That's not what Ms. Jones tells me." The woman edged forward, shrewd eyes watching Emory

Shéa MacLeod

like a hawk.

Every molecule in Emory's body was immediate on high alert. She only knew one Ms. Jones. "I'm sorry. Ms. Jones?"

The woman's eyes narrowed as if she believed Emory was lying. "Kabita Jones." She emphasized the last name as if somehow it would jog Emory's memory.

Oh, this was not good. Emory forced herself to appear relaxed. "Afraid not. Clearly, this Kabita Jones is mistaken. I'm sorry, I can't help."

The woman snorted. "Don't play coy with me," she snapped. She was now right up in Emory's personal space. How had that happened? Nobody moved that fast. A personal shield would give away the truth. Quickly, Emory sent out a mental call for help.

"Listen, witch," the woman in the fur coat hissed. She grabbed Emory's arm, her fingernails digging into pale flesh like claws. "I want that love potion, and I want it now," she snarled. Emory realized the woman's eyes weren't quite normal. The black pupils were probably twice the size they should be, and the thin rim of iris was red. Tomato red. Not exactly normal.

Emory yanked her arm, but the nails dug in, sending pain shooting up her arm. She tried not to wince, but her mouth was dry with fear. Who was this woman? She was not human, of that Emory was certain.

"Give it to me," the woman screeched, her face twisted into a caricature, "or else."

"Or else what?"

198

Both Emory and the woman stared at the open doorway, startled. Two women stood there, one blonde and one dark. Both looked like the Furies reborn, arms akimbo, faces wreathed in righteous anger.

"Let. Her. Go." The blonde paced forward, her eyes pools of black ink, a threat in every word.

Beside her, the other woman kept pace, her hair streaming in a gust of wind no one else could feel. Her eyes had turned silver, which was almost as freaky.

The woman in the fur coat stumbled backward, hands held up as if to ward them off. "I didn't mean no trouble," she all but whimpered. "I won't bother you no more." Gone was the haughty tone and elegant inflection. Sweat beaded her brow and upper lip.

"See that you don't," Emory snapped.

The woman whirled, her fur coat fanning dramatically behind her, and scurried out the door, slamming it behind her so hard the window pane next to it rattled ominously.

Emory heaved a sigh of relief. "Thanks, ladies. She was, uh, a little scary."

The blonde rushed forward and wrapped Emory in a hug before pulling back. Her eyes had bled from black back to their natural blue. "Are you okay?"

"I'm fine, Lene," she assured her best friend. "She just creeped me out. And gave me a nice set of claw marks as a memento." Emory showed them the set of bloody furrows raked through her skin, like blood on snow.

Lene made a distressed sound. "I'll get the med

kit." She hurried to the back room.

"What did that nasty bitch want, anyway?" Veri, the dark-haired witch, asked. Her eyes had returned to a soft, warm brown.

"She said she wanted a love potion. Claimed Kabita Jones sent her."

Veri snorted. "Please. That woman was a half-demon if ever I saw one. No way a demon hunter like Kabita Jones would send her our way. Not without warning, anyhow."

Emory knew she was right. Kabita Jones was the resident demon hunter of Portland, Oregon. She was also a natural born witch, like they were. And while she wasn't coven, preferring the life of a solitary witch, she was a friend. She'd have been more likely to kill the fur-wearing harpy than send her to Emory for a love potion.

"Kabita's in London, anyway," Lene said, returning from the storeroom with an old sewing basket in her hand. The basket had belonged to Emory's grandmother, except Emory didn't sew, so she'd converted it into a medical kit.

"True," Veri said thoughtfully as Lene pushed Emory into a chair and began rummaging in the med kit. "Likely the demon knew Kabita's name. What demon wouldn't? Decided to take a gamble. Lost big time."

"Thanks for rescuing me. Although I was hoping to get her out of here without giving away the fact that we can do magic." It was essential to keep things low key. Emory did not want the world knowing that not only was magic real, so were witches, and she and her friends were some of them. The last thing they needed was another installment of the Salem Witch Trials, only this time in Oregon instead of Massachusetts.

"Hey, what are friends for?" Veri said with a shrug. "Listen, everything under control here? Because I left the shop unmanned." Veri was not only her friend and fellow coven member, she also owned the lingerie store next door to Emory's shop, Healing Herbs.

Emory waved her off and closed her eyes as Lene silently cleaned and bandaged her arm. Emory pinched the bridge of her nose. A headache lurked just behind her eyes. Maybe she needed a dose of one of her own tinctures.

"Sorry about spilling the beans," Lene said, as she tucked the supplies back in the sewing basket. "It was just awful seeing that woman attacking you like that. And you not using any magic or anything?" She shook her head.

"Don't worry about it." Emory squeezed her hand. "It'll be fine. What's one half-demon woman who wants a stupid love potion, anyway?" But deep inside Emory had a feeling of foreboding.

She didn't have time to consider it further as the bell jangled above the door to the shop. She glanced up, half expecting the love potion demon lady to be back. Instead it was a young woman wearing an enormous pair of hot pink sunglasses and what was obviously a brown, pageboy wig. She glanced around nervously before approaching the counter.

She cleared her throat. "Emory Chastain?"

"That's me."

"My name is"—she hesitated—"Julia. Um, Zip

sent me."

An image flashed in Emory's mind of Zip, the former djinni who now inhabited the body of a human girl. They'd met only recently, but Zip's name carried a lot of weight thanks to who she was and her connections in the supernatural community. Not to mention her friendship with the local vampire hunter, Morgan Bailey, and Morgan's friend and boss, Kabita Jones.

Emory waved Lene off and rose to her feet, suddenly wary. "Zip sent you?"

Julia swallowed. "She said I should tell you she and Mick are, uh…" She pulled a slip of paper out of her pocket and glanced at it. "They're looking forward to dancing naked in the moonlight." She frowned. "I have no idea what that means."

Emory barely refrained from snickering. For some reason she couldn't fathom, Zip was convinced all witches danced naked in the moonlight and was constantly trying to get Emory to invite her and her boyfriend, Mick, over to do just that.

Emory gave Lene a look and, with a nod, Lene faded away. Emory waved her new client to the small alcove in the corner, where two comfortable chairs sat around a small, low table.

"Would you like to sit?"

Julia shook her head. "I don't have much time."

"Very well. How my I help you?" Emory kept her voice low and even. She had a feeling her newest customer was the kind who spooked easily.

Julie reached up and slowly slid her glasses off. Emory tried not to wince. The skin around the young woman's left eye was swollen and purple. Somebody had belted her good. Emory's palms itched with the need to punch whoever it was in some place a lot more sensitive than an eye.

"Who did that?" Emory couldn't help the question, though she realized it was invasive.

"My husband." Julia's voice was so soft, Emory could barely hear her.

"Does he do that often?"

Julia tilted her chin up a little, and Emory admired her struggle to be strong. Leaving abusive assholes could be difficult, but it was very brave.

"Yes."

Bastard. Emory swallowed her outrage. She had to remain calm. "What do you need me to do?" Hopefully the woman wouldn't ask her to put a curse on him. Although she was sorely tempted, Emory didn't want that shit bouncing back on her three-fold. There were rules when it came to magic. Whatever you put out there in the universe, that's what you got back. Including bad juju.

Julia cleared her throat and slid her glasses back on. "Hide me."

This time Emory did smile. "Now that I can do."

Her sandals slapped lightly against the wooden floor as she strode to a nearby display table. The footwear was her concession to working with the public, although she hated anything on her feet. It blocked her connection to Mother Earth. She missed the constant ebb and flow of energy between her and the planet. But the mundane world had its demands.

She grabbed a bar of soap from one table and then moved across the room. She selected a bottle of lotion from the glass shelves along the wall and returned to her waiting client.

"Take these," she said, handing Julia the items.

The young woman stared down at the lotion and soap. "Skin care products?" She frowned. "That's not going to hide me from my husband."

"Zip told you what I am, yes?"

She nodded. Emory couldn't see much of her expression behind the glasses. Did she believe what Zip told her?

"Then believe those bath products aren't ordinary."

"Okay." Julia's voice was shaky. "What do I do?"

"You have somewhere to stay? Somewhere your husband doesn't know about?"

"Yes, I—"

"No, don't tell me," Emory said holding up her hand. "It's better if I don't know. Just in case."

The other woman nodded. "All right."

"The minute you get to where you're staying, take a shower and wash with that soap. While you do, picture in your mind walking past your husband on the street and him not even noticing you. Then do the same with the lotion when you get out of the shower. Imagine you're slathering on an invisibility barrier. He looks at you, but he doesn't see you. Got it?"

Julia frowned. "Got it. Are you sure it will work?"

"Temporarily, yes. A few days only. Three. Four at most. So you need to get out of town as soon as possible." Emory opened the drawer behind the counter, took out a business card, and handed it to her.

"Fringe?" Julia asked, glancing down at the card.

"Isn't that a nightclub in downtown Portland? Don't…"—she glanced around, frightened— "…vampires hang out there?"

Emory hid her surprise. It was unusual to find an ordinary human who was aware of the vampire species. Most humans were stupid enough to think the whole idea sexy. It didn't appear Julia was one of them. Smart girl. "Yes. But I suggest going during the day. Go today if you can. Tomorrow at the latest. Speak to the bartender."

"Which one?"

Emory smiled. "There's only one. Tell him you need to disappear. He'll handle the rest."

"Can I trust him?"

Emory gave her a measured look. "Can you trust anyone?"

Julia sighed. "Good point. Thanks for… this."

"Good luck."

She nodded and scurried to the door, her sneakers squeaking slightly on the polished wood. The bell jangled as she slipped out. Emory heaved a sigh. A witch's work was never done.

Shéa MacLeod

A Note From Shéa MacLeod

Thank you for reading Kissed by Blood. If you enjoyed this book, I'd appreciate it if you'd help others find it so they can enjoy it too.

Please return to the site where you purchased this book and leave a review to let other potential readers know what you liked or didn't like about Kissed by Blood.

Book updates can be found at www.sheamacleod.com

Be sure to sign up for my mailing list so you don't miss out!
http://sheamacleod.com/mailing-list-2/

You can follow Shéa MacLeod on Facebook https://www.facebook.com/shea.macleod or on Twitter under @Shea_MacLeod.

Shea MacLeod

About Shéa MacLeod

Shéa MacLeod is the author of urban fantasy, post-apocalyptic, scifi, paranormal romances with a twist of steampunk. She also dabbles in contemporary romances with a splash of humor. She resides in the leafy green hills outside Portland, Oregon where she indulges in her fondness for strong coffee, Ancient Aliens reruns, lemon curd, and dragons.

Because everything's better with dragons.

Other Books by Shea Shéa MacLeod

<u>Sunwalker Saga</u>
Kissed by Blood
Kissed by Darkness
Kissed by Fire
Kissed by Smoke
Kissed by Moonlight
Kissed by Ice
Kissed by Eternity
Kissed by Destiny

<u>Sunwalker Saga: Soulshifter Trilogy</u>
Fearless
Haunted
Soulshifter

<u>Sunwalker Saga: Witch Blood Series</u>
Spellwalker
Deathwalker
Mistwalker (coming Summer 2016)

<u>Cupcake Goddess Novelettes</u>
Be Careful What You Wish For
Nothing Tastes As Good
Soulfully Sweet
A Stich in Time

<u>Viola Roberts Cozy Mysteries</u>
The Corpse in the Cabana
The Stiff in the Study
The Body in the Bathtub

<u>Notting Hill Diaries</u>
To Kiss a Prince
Kissing Frogs
Kiss Me, Chloe
Kiss Me, Stupid
Kissing Mr. Darcy

<u>Dragon Wars</u>
Dragon Warrior
Dragon Lord
Dragon Goddess
Green Witch
Dragon Corps

<u>Omicron ZX</u>
Omicron Zed-X: Omicron ZX prequel Novellette
A Rage of Angels

<u>Non-Series</u>
Angels Fall

Made in the USA
San Bernardino, CA
15 August 2016